D1479251

Send for the Saint

Two new adventures featuring that infamous *agent provocateur* Simon Templar, also known as the Saint.

By Leslie Charteris

DARE DEVIL	THE WHITE RIDER
THE BANDIT	X ESQUIRE

The Saint Series in order of sequence

Leslie Charteris'

Send for the Saint:
The Midas Double &
The Pawn Gambit

Two original stories by
JOHN KRUSE and DONALD JAMES

Adapted by
PETER BLOXSOM

PUBLISHED FOR THE CRIME CLUB BY
DOUBLEDAY & COMPANY, INC.
GARDEN CITY, NEW YORK
1978

All of the characters in this book
are fictitious, and any resemblance
to actual persons, living or dead,
is purely coincidental.

ISBN: 0-385-14138-6
Library of Congress Catalog Card Number 77-92210
Copyright © 1977 by Leslie Charteris
All Rights Reserved
Printed in the United States of America

First Edition in the United States of America

640900

Foreword

Whatever else may be said about the Saint stories which have been adapted from television scripts, it can at least be safely asserted that they are works of genius.

My authority for this statement is that all those which have been published hitherto were written up by Fleming Lee, who is a member of Mensa. And as everyone should know, membership in that highly elitist society is restricted to those who can prove an IQ in the top two percentile of the available statistics, which makes every Mensan officially a genius. On paper, at any rate.

Since the adaptations are also supervised and given their final vetting by myself, I am blushingly obliged to admit that I too am a Mensa member.

This volume introduces the first Saintly efforts of a new adapter, Peter Bloxsom. But to maintain a newly established tradition, I am glad to assure all readers that he too is a Mensan, whom I first met through our common membership.

So you have been warned. We may seem stupid to you, but we have certificates that say we aren't.

L C

Contents

I.

The Midas Double

CHAPTER 1

It was on a searingly hot August afternoon in 1950 that Simon Templar uncoiled his lean seventy-four-inch frame from the seat he had occupied for interminable hours in the creaking Parnassian Airways Dakota, and stepped down onto the tarmac of Athens Airport.

From above, as the plane had begun to sink into its droning, circuitous approach, Simon had looked down on the city with the same sense of unreality as he had felt on previous visits. There below, scarcely believable in their exact correspondence to all the tourist guidebook photographs, lay the monumental relics of the Old Greece; and there in less than comfortable juxtaposition with them were strewn the lesser glories of the New—those stark and faceless hotel and office blocks that were even then beginning to crawl like a blight across the green and ochre landscape. To anyone possessing, as the Saint possessed, a nodding acquaintance with the history and art of ancient Greece, the thought was inescapable that here was a nation whose architecture had deteriorated along with its Olympic athletes.

The thought being inescapable, Simon had not tried to escape it. He had merely sighed, and promised himself a longer visit before the rot went much farther.

On this occasion, he didn't mean to get on speaking terms with so much as a single Ionic column. He was purely and simply passing through, *en route* to London from Lebanon. In Beirut his attention had recently been occupied with one Elil Azziz, a large-scale flesh-trader and particularly unpleasant pustule on the face of humanity. Even the Saint had never been mixed up in a nastier bit of business; and even he had never come closer to death or had more cause to be grateful for the steel-spring nerves and reflexes with which a thoughtful providence had seen fit to equip him. In the end, he had succeeded in administering his own harsh yet poetic brand of justice to the excrescence in question, and in escaping not only with his own life but with some of the excrescence's more negotiable property, chiefly in the convenient form of banknotes. And the Saint now proposed to spend an indefinite period in London enjoying Mr Azziz's money on a lavish celebratory scale.

For the sake of accuracy, then, let it be recorded that he intended to remain on Greek soil for a period of just thirty-one minutes, this being the scheduled interval before the connecting flight. And let it be added that he was at that moment—aside from what might be called a certain constitutional readiness of the blood—definitely not in search of further Saintly adventure.

But he had failed to reckon with the persuasive charms of a certain Ariadne . . .

Despite the heat, no one could have looked more sublimely, insolently relaxed than Simon Templar as he sauntered into the airport passenger building. He had been entertaining himself by guessing at the occupations, preoccupations, and amorous propensities of his fellow passengers; and a faint smile hovered on his tanned piratical features as he wondered idly which of that motley crowd would contrive to smuggle the greatest weight, bulk, or value of contraband goods past the deceptively somnolent-looking Greek customs officers.

Simon had not been slow to notice the girl in the blue-and-gold airport staff uniform. She was armed with a clipboard on which she appeared to be keeping count as the incoming passengers filed past, and Simon had just drawn level with her when she spoke.

"Sir! One moment, please!"

The Saint turned, cocking a quizzical eyebrow, and looked into level wide-apart hazel eyes topped by a mop of dark curly hair. The eyes were set in a youthful elfin face, and the hair asserted itself defiantly against the restraint of the uniform-cap. Simon took in these and certain other details—including the way she filled the well-cut uniform—in a single, comprehensively appraising and approving glance, and replied with a seraphic smile, after scarcely an instant's hesitation:

"How can I help you? Only ask, and if it should lie within my power . . ."

"It is my pleasure to inform you that you are the two millionth passenger to pass through Athens Airport," said the girl, in the slightly formal tones of one who had rehearsed the sentence; and with a flourish of finality she made a large pencilled tick on the top sheet of the wad attached to her clipboard.

As she spoke she returned his smile and found her gaze met by a pair of the most amazingly clear blue eyes she had ever seen. Still more remarkable was the sublime innocence of their expression; but in them too, for a few moments, anyone who knew him well might have detected a faint, elusively mocking light as the Saint digested her announcement, weighed, considered, and formed a sceptical but open-minded judgement, before replying enthusiastically:

"What fun! This must be what my dear old Granny had in mind when she used to say I was fated to do something historic one day!"

"The management would like to make a small presentation," the girl continued. "And there's some champagne. Please come this way."

"Well . . ." Simon hesitated. "I don't want to risk missing my plane—"

"Please—it will take a few minutes only."

The Saint possessed, as he sometimes modestly reminded himself, a surprising number of natural assets that were invaluable in his hazardous freebooting trade. Not least among these aptitudes useful to any buccaneer with a hankering to stay in the business was his acute sense of the probable and the improbable—and when the notorious Simon Templar was stopped as the two-millionth passenger, or customer, or for that matter male visitor wearing shoes in a particular shade of brown . . . then it was entirely to be expected that the notorious Simon Templar should have his reservations concerning the probable truth of the claim.

But it was equally in character that he should have been swayed by his curiosity, and by the pleading in the eyes of a girl in a well-cut uniform. Wherefore the Saint replied, with an even more seraphic smile:

"All right. If you say so, I'll be delighted. Lead on, darling."

He followed her through a door marked *Official Use Only* in English and Greek, into a short corridor leading to another door. They passed through the second door into the open air.

"Are we having the champagne *al fresco?*" asked the Saint with interest. "Or—forgive my suspicious mind—have you been deceiving me?"

A gleaming new Rolls Royce in opulent purple stood nearby, a grey-uniformed chauffeur behind the wheel. At a nod from the girl, this worthy made some minimal movement of his body, and the Saint heard the abrupt, muffled cough of the starter, giving way instantly to the Rolls engine's well-bred, barely audible throb.

"Would you step into the car, please?" The girl's voice was still polite, but more matter-of-fact than before. The pleading had left her eyes.

"I think I'd rather not," Simon replied evenly. "I told you—I've got a plane to catch. If I'm going to make it, this is where I leave the party. Sorry. Now, if you'd really had some bubbly on the premises—"

He turned to go back through the same doorway, but even before he did so he knew with virtual certainty what he would encounter. The exact form taken by the expected obstruction was that of an extremely large Greek, dressed in the same grey chauffeur's livery and holding a squat automatic which he pointed unwaveringly at the Saint's chest.

"You will get into the car—Mr Templar," he rasped.

For a few moments the Saint soberly contemplated the bulky chauffeur-gunman, whom he instantly christened Big Spiro. In an automatic response—born of long experience of threats and physical struggles and mayhem and all manner of antagonists, large and small, who had pointed guns in his direction down the years—he rapidly measured the distance between them, pictured accurately the leap that would bring him within reach of Big Spiro's gunhand, gauged the other's probable speed of reaction and the strength in those massive arms—and concluded that for the time being he had little option but to do as he was told. He shrugged and obeyed the injunction, following the girl into the back of the car.

Big Spiro somehow managed to ease his own gigantic chassis through the same door and to wedge it into the seat beside the Saint's altogether more practical whipcord proportions without even a momentary deflection of the automatic protruding from his hamlike fist. Next he used the other ham of the pair to conduct an expert and thorough search of Simon's person; but he found nothing, for the Saint on his ordinary travels had long since ceased to go armed.

Simon was more than a little annoyed—in the first place with himself for allowing his curiosity to lead him so easily into a trap, but more particularly with whoever was behind the abduction.

"Just where are we going?" he demanded tersely as the big car glided silently away from the airport.

"You will see in good time," answered the girl. "And by the way—in case you should be so rash as to try to escape—all the car doors are electrically locked and only the driver can release them. Why not just relax? We do not mean you any harm, but if you attempt any heroics you will certainly be shot."

"We'd make a lovely couple, you and I," murmured the Saint, but if the girl understood she gave no sign.

She pressed a button in front of her, and a panel slid back to reveal a telephone. She picked up the handset, dialled, and after a moment's delay spoke softly into it. Simon had a sufficient smattering of Greek to understand.

"Ariadne reporting, sir. We have Mr Templar. We shall be with you by two-thirty."

He glanced at his watch and saw that it was two-fifteen.

"Just how long is this pantomime scheduled to last?" he inquired. A veneer of laziness in his voice thinly covered the iron-hard core of anger beneath. "Hours? Days?"

"Please, do not be impatient."

The mocking eyes danced like chips of blue steel.

"I've two main reasons for asking," he drawled. "One—before long I may very well tire of humouring your giant teddy-bear chum with the popgun. I've handled plenty of bigger dumb heavies in my time," he added, not entirely veraciously in view of Big Spiro's six feet eight and more than proportional width. "And two —do you realise that about now they'll be loading my suitcase into a London plane? I have—and I make no secret of it—certain eccentric habits. For example, every once in a while I change my socks. Now if I'm to be shortly separated from my spare Argylles . . . well, I'd prefer to avoid indelicacy, but my company could rapidly—"

"Your suitcase is in the boot of the car," interrupted Ariadne laconically; and Simon Templar blinked with something very like surprise, and mentally chalked up another point to his anonymous abductor.

With philosophic resignation, he sank farther back into the car's luxurious air-conditioned comfort and crossed one leg over the other, making the movements with slow, careful deliberation in deference to Big Spiro's trigger finger. No doubt that worthy colossus was under strict orders to deliver his prize alive and well, and no doubt he had been selected for his post with due care; yet however phlegmatically imperturbable he might appear, still a Greek is a Greek—quintessentially and forever a man of impulse and hot blood. And the Saint, knowing this well, saw no reason to take rash risks with the only skin he possessed.

He began to piece together what he knew or could deduce about the man from whom Ariadne and Big Spiro took their instructions. Who would want to kidnap the Saint? He had plenty of enemies with old scores to settle, but none in Greece that he knew of. For a moment his mind went back to recent events in Beirut; but on sober reflection he doubted if even the incendiary malevolence of Elil Azziz—especially bearing in mind the somewhat incapacitated condition in which the Saint had left him and his principal henchman that very morning—could have pursued him so swiftly.

As the purple Rolls whispered its insulated way through the Athens suburbs, groups of children gawped after it. Simon Templar, who had his moments of insight, had already categorised it as a far from discreet and inconspicuous vehicle. Not to mince words, it was the very latest model, announced only a month before; the colour was by special order, and Simon had already made a mental list of all the other custom features, among them the air-conditioning system, which together testified to the owner's flamboyant taste as well as to his ability and readiness to pay for every

conceivable luxury. Without doubt this was a wealthy and powerful man, someone used to impressing himself on the world, and
moulding his surroundings, and who took for granted that he
would always get his own way . . . It might be one of those repul-
sive *nouveau riche* tycoons who had grown newly fat on their lack
of scruples in the aftermath of the war and of the civil wars that
followed. And this was a man—the Saint felt a momentary grudging admiration—who worked with dazzling speed and efficiency;
at most he had had a few hours' advance notice of Simon's arrival
—and even for that he would have needed direct access to the airline's passenger list—yet the airport operation had been smooth
and unobtrusive, and the uniformed Ariadne had somehow been
installed with the connivance or toleration of genuine airport
staff.

That, more than anything, gave the Saint his clue. How could
this postulated potentate have worked that particular trick, short
of actually buying the whole airport?

A bell rang in Simon Templar's brain.

Of course—he could already own the airport. Or, very nearly
the equivalent in practice, he could own the airline—Parnassian—
that Simon had used. In which case . . . His lips came together in
a silent whistle. This was no minor tycoon; this was a big boy—
one of the biggest.

It was something of an inspired guess. But the Saint's inspired
guesses had so often proved uncannily accurate in the past that he
would have been more than mildly surprised now to find that he
had sired even a partial dud.

In the Saint's experience, powerful men sought him out either
in a blood-lust of revenge or in the hope of somehow employing
him towards their own further aggrandisement. Having mentally
ruled out the first, he plumped for the second.

"What makes your Mr Patroclos think he can buy me?" he
asked casually, and Ariadne's head swung suddenly around to face
him.

"How did you—"

The hazel eyes had widened.

"It could hardly be anyone else, sweetheart."

The Saint was conscious of the exaggeration; but he had something of the showman and the conjuror in his make-up, and like any producer of unexpected rabbits, he relished the effect upon his audience. Likewise he noted with satisfaction that when he had pronounced the name Patroclos—placing the stress correctly on the first syllable—even Big Spiro had shown visible surprise, and for all the Saint knew he might well have swallowed his dentures.

"Whoever was behind that stunt at the airport more or less had to own the place," Simon went on. "I'd guess you were on stage for only a few minutes, while I and the other passengers came through. But even that *could* have been long enough for you to be spotted by someone on the real airport staff."

"Unless they had been paid not to notice," Ariadne pointed out reasonably.

"And the customs men? No, this had to be more than ordinary bribery. This Johnny had to have really special influence. And I can't think of anyone in Greece who'd come anything like as close to that as our Diogenes, bless his puissant heart."

The girl hesitated for a moment.

"Well, it will do no harm to confirm your guesswork. Mr Patroclos wishes to see you on an important and confidential matter. But I cannot tell you what it is. You'll meet him soon enough."

CHAPTER 2

Diogenes Patroclos . . .

(The first name, which English speakers, for their own peculiar reasons, vocalise as *"Dye-odgen-eez,"* was pronounced by his compatriots as *"Thee-o-yen-ess,"* abbreviated by his familiars—by irreverent journalists to *"Thee-o."*)

The Saint was already scanning his card-index memory for everything he could remember about the man who was indisputably the wealthiest and most powerful living Greek, a man who controlled a vast and many-tentacled business empire, who was reputed to be among the world's shrewdest manipulators, and in whom the Saint, for certain reasons, had sometimes been tempted to take a sharpened interest.

He had read somewhere that Patroclos had come of a poor fishing family who had lived a few miles outside the capital. At fourteen, it was said (admittedly mostly by his critics) that he was the leader of a gang of young Athens pickpockets. At seventeen he was a seasoned merchant seaman, and besides piling up a tidy heap of drachmae, which he won in gambling with his shipmates, he had begun to get a grasp of the logistics of the business on which he later founded his fortune. His talent for figure-work and planning was exceptional; and he managed before long to manoeuvre himself into an office job with the same shipping company, and soon began climbing what is known as the management ladder. By the time he was twenty-one and fluent in three foreign languages he had already begun to amass capital by astute investment. At twenty-three or thereabouts, he launched out, so to speak, on his own, with one battered cargo steamer and an equally battered wharfside office in the Piraeus; and only a few years later he bought out his original employer. In the next twenty years he was in his element—assembling and consolidating a vast complex web of companies, mainly in shipping, air transport, investment, and insurance.

By all accounts Patroclos was a man of immense personal magnetism. His financial touch was a byword among his business contemporaries, and the timing of his acquisitions and divestments was generally regarded as next to uncanny. He was a Midas-figure who pulled strings and then—so it seemed—amused himself by watching the golden marionette-future respond exactly as he had willed.

That was Diogenes Patroclos, as pieced together from the Saint's mental file of the information scraps he had accumulated on the subject. But colossal and diversified as the Patroclos interests were, his first love, Simon knew, was still shipping. And it was the incidental uses of some of Mr Patroclos's ships in particular that had begun to arouse the Saint's speculation.

The Patroclos headquarters occupied one of the more salubriously situated, better camouflaged, and (as Greek estate agents or their counterparts anywhere in the world might have put it) more mature of the office blocks whose incursions Simon had lamented from the air. Which is simply to say that the physical centre of Mr Patroclos's aforementioned web of businesses was an edifice of manifestly superior quality, decently separated by a protective peripheral cushioning of verdure—including a few decorative citrus groves—from the nearest hubs of lesser commercial universes.

The Rolls disgorged its three passengers at the main entrance, and Ariadne ushered the Saint through the smoked-glass doors, where a plaque of suitably impressive dimensions depicted the chief constellations of the Patroclos cosmos. Big Spiro, his automatic no longer prominently on display, lumbered along behind; and the Saint flashed him a winning smile.

"Does Diogenes keep many other pet performing elephants?" he inquired with genuine interest.

Neither the mammoth nor Ariadne deigned to answer; and the Saint shrugged, and abandoned the attempt at polite conversation.

They proceeded into a large office labelled "D. Patroclos—General Staff" where male and female secretaries were busying themselves with typewriters and telephones. A male secretary got up after a few respectful words into a white telephone and opened the heavy double doors that led to Patroclos's inner office.

The room was spacious, though smaller than Simon had expected, sumptuously carpeted, and sparsely but superbly furnished in rich heavy browns with splashes of silver and glass here and there.

Patroclos stood up from his desk—a heavy, aggressive-looking man, exuding power like the room itself.

"Sir," began the girl, "this is Mr—"

"Out," snapped Patroclos. "I want no calls or interruptions."

He bundled her out and slammed the doors shut behind her; and the Saint meanwhile calmly installed himself in the mogul's reclining leather and silver chair, and rested his feet on the elegant walnut desk.

Patroclos turned and eyed the Saint penetratingly, making a lightning appraisal of the debonair ice-cool man who was lounging so insolently before him. And Patroclos saw a lean tanned buccaneer's face in which the lines of mirth and steel determination somehow coincided; a long relaxed frame that tapered from broad shoulders to the polished shoes that had taken defiant possession of the desk-top; and about the whole person of the Saint an indefinably yet almost tangibly dangerous swashbuckling air. And the Saint stared back at Diogenes Patroclos with ice-blue eyes that had narrowed fractionally as they observed the brusque treatment of Ariadne.

What the Saint saw was a broad, shortish, almost squat figure, a thick-set powerful body, a strong face, black musketballs of eyes under bushy black eyebrows, and still plenty of matching hair atop the somewhat cro-magnon head. Patroclos was wearing a blue serge suit, stiff gleaming linen, and a ring with a diamond in it as big as a cob-nut.

The Saint saw all these things. And then his anger surfaced.

"Dio, old toad," he began, in a voice thinly edged with silk, "you have made a serious blunder. I am about to give you a graphically detailed rundown on your antecedents, your future prospects of happiness, and a few of the unpleasant experiences which I've decided will have to befall you. Besides which I expect to describe—if I can bring myself to look at you—some of the many repellent features of your gross person."

Patroclos inclined his head slightly and studied the Saint for a few moments longer.

"So you are the famous Simon Templar," he said, baring his teeth in a mechanical half-smile. "I am very pleased to meet you."

"The pleasure's all yours," said the Saint evenly. "I never liked very much of what I'd heard of you, Dio, and now I've seen you I like you even less."

"Naturally you are angry," said Patroclos in a conciliatory tone. "Your journey has been interrupted. You have been brought here against your will. You have been threatened. I too, in your place, would be angry—very angry." He made a pantomime gesture of expanding his chest and throwing his arms wide as if breaking out of bondage. "But—"

"I am much more than very angry," the Saint cut in. "If there's one species of humanity I abhor above all others it's a bloated plutocratic string-puller who calmly assumes that there's nothing and nobody on earth his money can't buy. I am so angry that I'm on the point of taking you apart piece by piece and scattering the bits in the Aegean—except that I'd have a conscience about poisoning the fish. Afterwards I might just start on your maritime operations. There have been nasty whispers lately about some of your cargoes and their destinations, and I'm enough of an old-fashioned puritan to get hot under the collar about such things. All in all, from where I sit, your future looks distinctly less than rosy."

The black eyes flashed and the heavy brows swooped. Diogenes Patroclos controlled himself with difficulty.

"Yes, yes," he said hurriedly, "you are a remarkable man. I have heard many tales of your exploits. I do not doubt that you could do me damage. But I do not desire your enmity. Templar, you are a man I admire. Yes—I, Diogenes Patroclos! I possess money, power, organisations, everything. But you—you are a man of daring . . . we would say a *klephtes*—a robber-hero—"

Simon interrupted.

"Now get this straight. Whatever I may be—or may have been in the past—I was just now on my way to London. I was taking a well-earned holiday. Which you have had the temerity, the super-heterodyne gall, to interrupt with your—"

"Yes, yes. It will all be made good. But please—you are here now. Listen to me. I need help—and you are the best man in the world to give it. I will pay a lot of money."

"Dio, you're up a gum-tree. Your information is faulty. I work for myself. I don't take commissions under pressure."

"The pressure was regrettable—but a temporary expedient only. I give you my word, Templar—if you reject my proposition you will be free to leave at once and no harm will be done to you."

"Goodbye, then," said the Saint, getting up from Patroclos's chair.

"Wait! You will change your mind when you hear. This must interest you, a man of your experience, your abilities. I am being impersonated, Templar! No, a better word, *duplicated!*"

"Disgusting!" said the Saint with feeling.

"Think of a carbon copy, a photograph, so accurate in every detail as to be identical. There are two of me, Templar, two!"

"The thought quite turns my stomach," said the Saint, with an elaborate shudder.

For a few moments the bullet eyes smouldered and the muscles tensed and untensed around Patroclos's prominent jaw.

"That is your only comment?"

The Saint sighed.

"Apart from the obvious—that it's impossible."

"So we agree. Impossible."

"Those old fairty-tales about perfect doubles are tactual balancy."

"Yes, yes—to imitate clothes, that is simple. Mannerisms, even. But beneath them is the man—*me!*"

"Quite," said the Saint, becoming bored.

"Me! Unique. Unrepeatable! These lines—" Patroclos thrust his jaw forward and outlined its contour with a hairy hand. "No man can have these things without being *me!*"

"Right. Case solved. You can put my cheque in the post."

Patroclos moved up very close to Simon and took a deep breath. The black eyes bulged.

"But, Templar, though we both know it is impossible, *there is such a man.*"

The Saint cocked an eyebrow. "You've seen him, of course?"

"No. But friends say to me, 'I saw you last week in Paris.' But I tell them I have not been in Paris. I have been here in Athens."

The Saint's interest, against his will, was beginning to be
aroused. He meant exactly what he had said about the proposition
that any man could have a "perfect double." The variability of
humankind, in behaviour, voice, and appearance, was so infinitely
manifold that two people in practice rarely turned out to be even
approximate doubles. And yet, here was a man seriously claiming
such an impersonation.

"I find entries in my bank statements," Patroclos continued,
"showing I have made purchase of a new car, a piece of jewellery,
when I have made no such purchase!"

"Did you ask to see the cheques?"

"Of course. My own signature! Indistinguishable! But I did not
sign them . . . Now, listen. I have houses, apartments, offices. All
over the world. This man uses them! Wherever I am not, he is!
He knows my every movement."

"Interesting," the Saint mused.

"And for every suit I possess, it seems he has had made another,
identical!" Patroclos was becoming emotional; the voice rose and
fell excitedly; the words came out in clusters, a few at a time,
under immense pressure. "I tell the London Police, I am being
impersonated. They must find the man quick. A week later they
arrest *me!*"

Simon laughed.

"Yes . . . ha-ha!" Patroclos went on. "But I am proceeding to a
big meeting. I tell the police this. But no. I must go first to
Scotland Yard. They see my passport . . . all the things. At last
they are convinced. I am the real Patroclos. I may go. So I precipitate myself to this meeting. But what is this? It is finished without
me."

"You're not telling me," Simon said in amazement, "that he—"

"Yes! This masquerader has been there! I was then to learn
that he had blocked a deal I was planning. In place of it he had
negotiated another."

"Now that really is interesting," said the Saint softly.

"So, the impossible happens. But Templar, even that was just
the beginning. Since then there have been many such deals."

The Saintly blue eyes searched the mogul's face.

"What kind of deals?"

Patroclos hesitated.

"Shipping. All shipping."

"Your favourite game . . ." Simon said slowly, his brain struggling to make a connection. "Were the deals successful?"

"Very successful. But not deals I would have made. Unprincipled deals."

"In what way?" asked the Saint, without much doubt about the answer.

Patroclos hesitated again.

"Heroin to the United States. Arms to . . . certain powers, supplies and aid to others. Earlier, Templar, you spoke of your heat under the collar at these things. You had heard rumours—yes? But no proof . . ."

"The American authorities are pretty certain that your ships have been carrying these cargoes. Admittedly they've yet to catch you red-handed."

"But that is the point! It is not *me*. My ships are being used—yes . . . but only under the direction of this—this double!"

The Saint smiled.

"And you want me to catch him?"

"I will pay you twenty thousand pounds if you do."

"Well, I won't," said the Saint firmly. "I'm on holiday. I told you."

Patroclos looked crestfallen.

"But, Templar, the matter does interest you. Obviously. And twenty thousand pounds—that is a lot of money. Then why—"

Simon sighed.

"Dio," he began with exemplary surface patience, "a little while ago I explained very clearly that I disliked your approach. I told you I was annoyed. I still am annoyed. You messed up my plans, and I was contemplating various ways of making your life uncomfortable in return. But since this repulsive-looking *Doppelgänger* of yours seems to be doing the job pretty well on his own, I'm willing to forego the pleasure of pinning your ears back myself. Now if you'll just see that I get on the next plane to London, I'll be generous and forget what a nuisance you've been."

And the Saint pushed through the double doors into the outer office, leaving a seething Patroclos behind him.

CHAPTER 3

He found Ariadne sheafing through some files.

"Darling," he said, "you arrange things so cleverly. I want a seat on the next flight to London. Mr. Patroclos and I have concluded our business, you might say."

The girl looked up; and not by so much as a flicker of an eyebrow did she acknowledge what she saw beyond the Saint's dangerous form—her boss's squarer, squatter physique framed in the doorway as he shook his head at her vigorously.

"There isn't another flight until the morning, I'm afraid," she told him with only a fractional hesitation.

"Really?" Simon was bluntly sceptical.

"Really," she said more firmly. "But since we do have a suite booked for you at the Grande Bretagne tonight . . . ."

"Oh, we do? On the house, I suppose?"

"Naturally."

The Saint reflected.

"Hmm . . . I suppose a night in Athens could have its compensations."

Ariadne looked relieved to have no further argument on her hands.

"The morning flight is at ten-fifteen. I will make the booking now, and you can exchange your existing ticket at the airline desk in the morning. Now I will order the car to take you to the hotel."

Simon flipped a hand in a goodbye gesture and strolled out, arriving at the front door simultaneously with the Rolls. He had kept his cool composure throughout, but during the drive to the hotel he reflected on the encounter with an obscure feeling of dissatisfaction.

Patroclos was right on one point: it was a fascinating problem, and one that could hardly have failed to arouse the Saint's professional curiosity. But Simon Templar danced to no man's tune, but only to the music of his own individual ideals—which mainly concerned justice, and a comfortable living for buccaneers who took on the dangerous task of administering it. It had always been so with him and probably always would. Therefore he had refused the job, exactly as he had meant to do.

And yet he felt an undefined disquiet, as though he had nonetheless been manipulated in some way that eluded his grasp. Somewhere deep in the underlayers of his subconscious mind a tiny premonitory bell was tinkling out the merest ghostly half-echo of a warning; but it was somehow too far off and too subtle to be grasped and interpreted, though the Saint creased his brow with the effort for several minutes.

He had not seen, did not guess, how abruptly the thunderclouds fell from Patroclos's features as soon as he was alone. Nor had he seen how swiftly those same features formed themselves into an expression of triumphant cunning that would have made Machiavelli look like a dewy-eyed innocent. Nor could he have any knowledge of the brief phone call that Patroclos next made. Had he known of these things, he would also have known at once that Diogenes Patroclos was even more astute than he had supposed.

The Grande Bretagne was one of the institutions of Athens, and there was nowhere Simon would rather have stayed. The reception clerk, a thin sallow youth, was evidently expecting him.

"Ah yes, Mr Templar. One of our best suites. Would you sign, please."

While the Saint was signing the name whose syllables were known with approximately equal unpopularity to both the underworld and the police forces of several countries, the sallow clerk produced a long envelope.

"This contains your papers, Mr Templar. They were sent from the airport."

He reached down and handed the Saint a second smaller envelope. "And this was left for you a short while ago."

Simon opened the second envelope, and found inside it an air ticket for London and a handwritten note which said simply:

*The girl was lying. A flight leaves at 5.30. You will be well ad-
vised to be on it, and not to stay here where you may be
tempted to involve yourself in matters that do not concern
you.*

While he was reading the anonymous message, Simon became
aware of two thick-set Greeks wearing off-white suits and dark
glasses who had appeared at either side of him.

"You understand?" said the first, flashing a mouthful of gold
teeth in the Saint's general direction. "A car is waiting outside to
take you to the airport."

"How thoughtful," said the Saint. "But a bit premature. I'm
leaving in the morning. Ask the driver to come back then."

"No. You must leave now. Patroclos may try again, and you
may change your mind."

"So just pick up your bag," said the other Greek, pressing a gun
into Simon's ribs in a manner that made it difficult to ignore.

The Saint's eyes narrowed fractionally and the muscles of his
jaw tightened. To be abducted at gunpoint twice in one day was
coming close to being repetitious; and the Saint found that he was
already tired of the game. But Big Spiro was one thing, and two
amateurs in an open hotel lobby were quite another. The Saint
shrugged, picked up the suitcase, and strode rapidly towards the
exit.

"Mr Templar . . . !" The clerk stared after him in blank puzzlement. But his stare grew more pop-eyed still as he watched the
Saint go into action.

Gold-teeth's gun, if he had one, was not in his hand. That was
a mark of amateurism, and a serious mistake. And if Simon
Templar knew anything, he knew how to take advantage of the
mistakes of the ungodly.

When he began striding towards the door, Gold-teeth and his
companion with the gun immediately followed, hurrying to keep
up with the Saint's long strides.

And the Saint suddenly stopped dead.

What happened next was etched into the fascinated hotel
clerk's memory in graphic detail.

There were two *"wmph"*s in perfect unison as the big suitcase slammed its outer corners symmetrically into the midriffs of Gold-teeth and his colleague; and then five steely fingers fastened with uncanny speed on the wrist attached to the gun-holding hand, and the gun fell to the ground. Simon kicked it away, and in the same instant the outside edge of his right hand arced up suddenly from out of nowhere and chopped devastatingly into the narrow target formed by Gold-teeth's upper lip where it joined his nose. Gold-teeth reeled back gasping from the back-handed blow whose surprising incapacitating power the Saint had learned years before in Shanghai; and with the point of his left shoe the Saint kicked the other man hard in the shins—a manoeuvre of less exotic prov-enance which also had its moments of usefulness. The reflex im-pulse to bend over and clutch at the wounded shin in these cir-cumstances is a strong one, and unfortunately for him, the gunman yielded to it. As his head came down, it met Simon's fist travelling rapidly in the opposite direction in a long looping up-percut that connected with the point of his chin and sent him off into the land of dreams.

As he staggered and began to fall, the Saint steered him towards the crumpling Gold-teeth until a final shove brought their two heads into loud collision, and both slumped to the ground to-gether with no further interest in the proceedings.

Simon smoothed back his hair, recovered the gun, and said to the open-mouthed clerk: "Sorry about that. Would you arrange to have them taken away? I suggest the garbage collectors. Oh, and would you have a porter take my bag to my room?"

And the Saint strolled into the hotel bar.

Over an ice-cool lager, he reflected. Somebody was obviously very anxious to prevent his involvement in the Patroclos affair; and if the Saint disliked being pressured into a certain line of ac-tion, he disliked even more being warned off.

Twenty minutes later he paid off a taxi in front of the Patroclos HQ building and strode past the receptionist and through the outer office, waving to Ariadne; then he opened the big double doors to reveal Patroclos at his desk.

"Templar!"

"I've thought things over," said the Saint simply.

"And changed your mind? Splendid. I knew you would not be

able to resist opposing yourself to the cleverness of this impersonator . . ."

"Is there anything else I should know?" asked the Saint.

"Yes. There is my codebook. This man or his agents have been
to my safe!"

Simon nodded.

"I figured as much when you said he'd been able to use your
cheques. But what's in the codebook?"

Patroclos made an all-embracing gesture.

"Everything crucial. Details of my entire business empire: details which I need in order to direct operations. No one else is permitted to have access to all of these details together—none of my
employees, even the most senior and trusted. But *he* has them!
Plus—most important of all—the codes I use to communicate
vital instructions to my key executives."

"Which you immediately cancelled, I trust," said the Saint.

"Naturally I attempted to. But he is clever, Templar—very
clever. He had already contacted—this you will not believe—he
had already notified my major companies that an impostor is at
large and would attempt to change the codes! He tells them in my
name! They are to ignore any such attempt—they must respond
only to the established codes!"

"And I suppose you've no other copy of the codes?"

Patroclos sighed. "For security reasons, I kept only one book. I
realise now this was bad security. *He* has the codes and *he* can
give vital instructions, but I cannot even cancel his orders. Do you
not see what this means, Templar?"

"I think I'm beginning to get the picture," said the Saint
mildly.

The black eyes bulged and the hairy hands gesticulated excitedly as Patroclos continued.

"This is the crucial step in taking over my businesses—my entire life. He *becomes* me. He acquires a greater claim to my existence than I myself! He overtakes me, turns *me* into the impostor.
He forces me out and takes my place. So—Templar—please find
this masquerader and get back my codebook."

"And where do I start?"

"London."

"London?" The Saint raised an eyebrow.

"It should not be so inconvenient for you. You were on your way there. Now you can continue your journey. Next week I have an important series of meetings in London. He will almost certainly be intending to be there. Your job is to find him—forestall him. And, Templar," he added with some further eyebulging and gesticulating, "most important—get back my codebook. Quickly!"

"I'll be on my way in the morning," said the Saint.

"There is a flight at half past five," Patroclos said.

"Ariadne didn't seem to think so earlier."

"So. Perhaps she forgot—this is Tuesday. There is an evening flight. I will tell her to arrange your ticket."

"Oddly enough," said the Saint with quiet thoughtfulness, "I've got one already."

CHAPTER 4

Simon Templar arrived in London in the small hours and went straight to the compact mews house behind Queen's Gate that had served his needs so well for several years. Its position and construction offered certain natural advantages—which was why he had chosen it in the first place—and the Saint had added a unique range of refinements, including some highly unorthodox gadgetry that had proved invaluable in his dealings with both the underground and the law.

Outside the street door he consulted a tiny light-bulb which was tucked away in a hidden recess; and with some further precautions he went in. Some quick checks confirmed that no one had been in the house in his absence. These were merely routine actions that had become semi-automatic for a privateer like the Saint with an instinct for survival.

He slept until nine, which he regarded as a moderately civilised hour at which to rise, swing a pair of Indian clubs vigorously for a few minutes, shower, and consume quantities of bacon, eggs, toast, and coffee. The Saint did all these things, and in that order; and then, fit and ready to punch the world on the nose, he sallied forth.

The first object on which his energies impinged was the long-nosed cream-and-red Hirondel in the garage. Simon spent a few minutes preparing it for the road, and after re-setting his various household devices he snaked the big car through the traffic to the offices of the *Daily Express*, where a sub-editor on the paper, Joe Daly, had often helped out in the past by allowing him access to files and photographs.

Joe was in cheerful form as always, and the Saint grinned as the short square figure appeared and slapped him on the back.

"Simon, you old son of a gun!" he exclaimed in his chirruppy brogue. "How's business? Been keeping the nose clean then, I see," he added, referring to the lack of recent news stories about the Saint's exploits.

"I've been out of the country for a while, Joe. What can you give me on Diogenes Patroclos?"

"Patroclos? Old golden guts?"

"The same. Joe, I'd be obliged if you'd show me what you've got in the photo library."

They went together into the long room that housed the paper's main collection of personal data. Daly rummaged in a cabinet.

"Strictly against the rules, this, Simon, y'know. Ah, here we are, Diogenes Patroclos." Daly pulled out a hefty file and gave it to Simon. "And there's references to a whole string of his companies —you can have a look at the files of them if you like. Mostly pictures of aircraft and ships, as I remember."

"Thanks, Joe. Just now it's the man himself that I'm interested in," explained the Saint as he riffled through the photos.

Daly peered over his shoulder.

"Ugly bugger, isn't he. What's he been up to?"

"You tell me," said the Saint.

Daly looked reflective.

"Wait—there was something. His ships've been carrying some dodgy cargoes lately. There was some rumbling here and there about it."

The Saint nodded.

"I'd heard that much. But it never made the papers, did it?"

"We tried to work up a feature, but the old man said let it ripen a bit first."

"What about women?" the Saint asked, still thumbing through the photographs.

"The man's a monk. Only thing he takes home are bits of glass."

"Glass?"

"Tinkle-tinkle, you know. Stuff you drink out of. He's got one of the best collections in the world. Antique goblets—all that sort of thing . . ."

The Saint had stopped and extracted two photos from the file.

"Joe—look at these."

Daly took them, glanced at the pictures, and then read the description on the reverse.

"Diogenes Patroclos presenting the Out Islands Yachting Trophy—Nassau. . . . Diogenes Patroclos party-going in Lisbon. So what?"

"Read the dates when they were taken," suggested the Saint. Daly read the date stamped in the corner on the back of each print.

"Tenth July, 'forty-nine . . . Tenth July, 'forty-nine." Daly frowned, puzzled. "Well, he couldn't have been in two places at once . . . Wait a minute, the photos must have been taken a few hours apart—Nassau in the afternoon or evening, Lisbon later on . . . No, that's no good, no plane would get him there that fast. Must be a misprint."

Simon nodded thoughtfully.

"Mind if I borrow these two?"

"Help yourself—just don't flash 'em around on your way out."

The Saint was willing to admit to himself that this duplicate tycoon had him, at that moment, completely perplexed. He was as reluctant to believe in the possibility of perfect impersonation as in the existence of talking dogs; yet here was this Patroclos double, seemingly breaking all the rules. And the two photographs appeared to clinch the issue. Simon's reasoning on that had followed much the same course as Joe Daly's: two photos had been taken no more than a few hours apart, and each showed unmistakably a man who appeared to be Patroclos; but it was an inescapable fact that no aircraft could possibly have flown him from Nassau to Lisbon in those few hours. In any case there was a time lag of several hours, which made it all the more inconceivable that he could have travelled from one engagement to the other.

After leaving the *Express* building Simon drove to Berkeley Square, where Patroclos had his London house. Simon cruised around the square until he came to the number Patroclos had given him. And then, to put it mildly, he blinked his eyes in disbelief.

True, the Patroclos house was one of the most expensive and elegant residences in that expensive and elegant quarter. That was exactly as the Saint had expected. But what he had not expected was to see Diogenes Patroclos and Ariadne getting out of a silver Bentley and going into the house.

For perhaps a minute, the Saint stared after them at the closed door. They had given no sign of noticing his presence, but he had been close enough to them to see that the likeness, if they were doubles of the real Patroclos and Ariadne, was incredible. Certainly, the Saint mused, from a distance of a few feet it was utterly convincing visually. Whether the effect could be sustained at closer quarters and when voices and mannerisms could be studied, remained to be seen. The Saint had every intention of taking a close look at the two of them, but first there was one obvious check that had to be made.

He drove back to Manson Place and phoned Athens.

After the usual delay he was connected with the Patroclos HQ. He asked for Patroclos, and Ariadne came on the line.

"No, of course we are not in London. We are here in Athens."

"But I've just seen someone here could be him."

"That is impossible. Mr Patroclos is here in his office."

"Let me speak to him," said the Saint.

Ariadne hesitated.

"He is in conference. He gave strict instructions that he was not to be disturbed."

"Get him to the phone—now," Simon said flatly, "or I quit the job."

There was a moment's silence.

"All right," Ariadne replied. "But he will be very angry. And you will have to wait while I interrupt the meeting."

After some delay Simon heard Patroclos's familiar accents on the line.

"Templar—I am told you have seen the impostor. Why are you wasting time telephoning, instead of watching him?"

"I just wanted to be quite sure," explained the Saint, "that it *was* the impostor I saw."

"I am here in Athens. If you have seen the impostor, it should make your job easier. Now I am very busy. Please do not waste my time telling me that I am being impersonated. That I already know. Goodbye."

There was a definitive *clunk* on the line, followed by a silence that effectively terminated all argument.

The Saint hung up and remained wrapped in thought for many minutes afterwards.

However, he had certain other private interests of some insistence with legitimate demands on his time, so that it was not until the evening that his meditations reverted entirely to the problems of Diogenes Patroclos, as his peregrinations took the Hirondel again through Berkeley Square. And it happened that he was cruising past Patroclos's house just as an easily recognisable "society" couple in evening dress got out of a chauffeur-driven car. They rang the bell; the door opened, and they were admitted at once, but not so quickly that Simon missed catching a glimpse of someone shaped like Ariadne who was doing the reception. By the time he had a chance to stop without creating a block of honking traffic, another evening-dressed and equally publicised couple arrived and were admitted by Ariadne's double in the same manner. And then the Saint's eyes widened in amazement as he realised the extent of the fake Patroclos's sheer barefaced audacity.

The impostor was giving a party.

CHAPTER 5

For a few blissful minutes, the Saint sat in the car and savoured the full rich succulence of the situation. He watched as more guests—a dozen or so more—arrived. And then he spoke philosophically calming words to himself and went home to change into a more suitable costume than he was wearing.

Thirty minutes later, immaculately tuxedoed for the occasion, he knocked at the door of the Berkeley Square house. It was opened by the girl who looked like Ariadne; and the likeness was passable enough; but Simon was certain that this was not the girl he had met in Athens.

"Ariadne!" cried the Saint, with a complete show of spontaneous warmth. "And looking more beautiful than ever!"

The girl's eyes flickered with puzzlement.

"Have we met somewhere?"

"Monte Carlo. Simon Templar. We shared a langouste at the Hotel de Paris, I seem to remember."

"I . . . I think you must be mistaken," said the girl slowly.

Simon's brain was racing to make her reaction add up to some kind of sense. If she was impersonating the real Ariadne, he reasoned, surely she should be bluffing it out?

"Oh dear, forgotten incident, are we?" Simon did his best to look hurt. "Well, never mind—just tell Dio I'm here, would you?"

Ariadne Two flushed and hesitated; she must have known that the name Simon Templar appeared nowhere on the guest list, but she was reluctant to turn him away in case Patroclos himself had invited this tall and insolently handsome man and forgotten to let her know.

"I suppose it's all right," she said reluctantly. "You'd better come in."

"Righto," said the Saint, who was already halfway into the hall.

His keen glance took in the crystal chandeliers and bracket-lights, the magnificent gilt mirror, the marble floor and columns, the elegant carved staircase. Georgian classic at its best. Coats and furs bulged from the cloaks recess behind the front door, and an upper-class babble of voices issued from the drawing-room into which Simon followed the dubious-faced Ariadne Two.

About twenty people were standing about in typical party groups, drinking champagne and talking—and making more noise about both activities than was strictly necessary. Most of the guests were instantly recognisable, as Simon had already noted, as bigwigs of one sort or another—cultural, social, financial, or in some cases all three.

"Do you know anyone?" Ariadne Two asked.

"Probably," replied the Saint. "I don't see Dio, though."

"He's busy at the moment. But I'll tell him you're here."

Ariadne Two beckoned over the footman with a tray of drinks; and then, with a last uncertain glance at the Saint's innocent features, she disappeared through a door at the far end of the room.

Simon sampled the fine champagne appreciatively while his eyes absorbed the scene. Next to him a group were conversing loudly, trying to make themselves heard above the general hubbub.

"Well, you know Dio," a famous merchant banker was explaining. "Once he gets his claws into a man . . ."

"Don't we know!" chuckled another well-known financier. "Rends him limb from limb. What exactly did he do to this Kellner?"

"Sold the company. And him along with it—bound by contract for the next five years. Sold it to a firm of East End bookmakers, if you please!"

"Ha! Sold him into slavery, eh?"

"Exactly!"

"Marvellous!" put in the large operatic contralto who was part of the same group.

"Good old Dio," said a younger, very decorative woman in the group. "Never changes, does he?"

The cue was too perfect for the Saint to resist.

"Oh, I don't know," he remarked. "Wouldn't you say he'd changed a bit recently?"

Six pairs of eyes turned to look at the newcomer; and one of the financiers asked, "How d'you mean?"

Simon hesitated.

"I'm not exactly sure. I can't put my finger on it somehow. There's something . . . Maybe his appearance. Haven't you noticed?"

"Well, none of us gets any younger," suggested the more ornamental of the women, with an appreciatively appraising glance at the Saint's youthfully lean and elegant form.

"I don't mean he's aged, exactly," he explained. "Just . . . changed."

"Well, *I* haven't noticed it," put in the large contralto decisively, as if that must be the end of the matter.

The Saint shrugged.

"Oh well, it was just an impression. Perhaps I'm wrong." And then, as Ariadne Two appeared at his side and touched him on the arm, he added, "Will you excuse me?" and followed the girl through the far doorway.

"Mr Patroclos would like to talk to you privately," she explained, as they passed through a small communicating room into the library beyond.

The room was fully pine-panelled, its walls lined with sunken bookshelves stuffed full of leather-bound volumes. Two big showcases full of choice glassware dominated one side of the room; and from a solid compact mahogany desk in one corner, the double of Diogenes Patroclos stared at Simon Templar with piercing interest.

Ariadne Two closed the door softly, leaving them alone.

The likeness was incredible. To any ordinary observation this *was* the same Diogenes Patroclos as the Saint had met in Athens: the same heavy figure, the same powerful set to the head and jaw, and the same sallow Greek complexion, the same bushy black brows and musketball eyes. And yet, to the Saint's acutely perceptive scrutiny, there were minute, infinitesimal differences, which were well-nigh impossible to analyse—perhaps a fractional discrepancy here in the sweep of the hair, or there in a line or two of the face—but which nevertheless added up to just enough of an identifiable distinction to make the Saint feel fairly sure he would now be able to tell Patroclos One and Patroclos Two apart.

He went straight to Patroclos Two, hand extended.

"Dio. Good to see you!"

"Templar! What brings you here at this hour?"

The voice and handshake were noncommittal; Patroclos Two was not refusing to recognise the Saint, as the girl had done, but neither was he playing it up to the hilt. He was waiting and watching. But Simon marvelled at the double's achievement with the voice, as much as with the appearance: again the difference from the man in Athens was so slight and elusive that no one would have detected it who was not listening for it—and listening with an ear as acute as the Saint's.

"I was just passing," Simon replied. "There seemed to be a party going on, so I thought you wouldn't mind if I dropped in and said hullo. How was Athens?"

"Not good. You know—the political situation." Patroclos made a seesaw movement in the air with one hand. "Anyhow, you are welcome. You look well."

"I hope so. But I was beginning to wonder. Ariadne gave me the cold shoulder just now. She didn't seem to recognise me at all."

Patroclos Two shrugged.

"Ariadne meets a lot of people . . . Now, will you have a drink? A cigar?"

The Saint accepted a Peter Dawson, declined a jumbo-size cigar, and settled into a deep leather chair. The Patroclos double watched.

"What have you been doing with yourself, Templar?" he asked casually. "Since Monte Carlo?"

And he blew a cloud of heavy cigar smoke into the room. Evidently this copy-Patroclos was in no hurry. For the present he could afford to bide his time, waiting for the Saint to explain his presence. But still the black bullet eyes watched.

"Oh, I've been scouting around—you know, finding a good piece here and there. Nothing very energetic. But as a matter of fact"—here Simon adopted a confidential tone—"and this is actually the reason I wanted to see you, I *may* have found you another Millefiori."

Patroclos Two's eyebrows swooped in a sharp reaction.

"Have you really?"

Simon nodded. He had begun with the idea of getting into the impostor's house and then playing it by ear from there; and now the imps of devilry were urging him on to see how far he could get this impostor out on a limb.

"A matching piece to the one I sold you in Monte Carlo," he said, wondering if he was overreaching himself. "You *have* still got it, I hope?"

Patroclos Two hesitated for a moment, and then the hint of a crafty smile crossed his features as he beckoned the Saint over to one of the glass-cabinets.

"See for yourself." He indicated the cabinet.

"Ah, yes . . ." Simon began, seeing no easy way out of the trap that he himself had set; and Patroclos Two's voice cut in suddenly.

"Which one?"

Simon made a last attempt to carry it off.

"I'm hardly likely to forget!" he laughed.

"Which one?" repeated Patroclos, watching him, hawklike.

With an air of supreme confidence, the Saint pointed.

"That one."

Patroclos Two nodded thoughtfully, as if to say that matters stood much as he had expected, and he moved back to sit behind the desk again.

"I am glad to see that you have done some homework, Templar. But . . . not . . . quite . . . enough. That piece came from the Andersen collection. I bought it in Copenhagen two years ago."

"Well, I never," said the Saint, scratching his head. "You know, Dio, I could have sworn . . ."

"Enough games!" The voice cut across the room like a whiplash. "We have never met before, and you never sold me anything. Now what do you want?"

And the Saint knew that the masks were off. The bluff had failed.

"You should be able to guess what I want," he said in a level voice.

Patroclos Two regarded him scowlingly from under the bushy black brows.

"You think I might make a deal with you, is that it?"

"Possibly," said the Saint slowly. "It might just save your bacon."

The double eyed him impassively for a few moments.

"Sit down, Templar," he invited.

Simon sat down again in the leather chair; and the dancing blue eyes under his quizzically tilted brows looked more innocent than ever.

"When Ariadne says you are here," Patroclos Two began, "I say to myself, what is the famous, the notorious Saint doing in my house? It was very puzzling to me. At first."

"At first?" queried the Saint.

"My dear Templar." Patroclos Two beamed. "It is very clear. You have heard that I am being impersonated. It has been kept out of the newspapers, yes—but you have your own contacts, your own sources of information—perhaps even in Scotland Yard. So—you know about this masquerader. As an adventurer, naturally you are intrigued. And you resolve to investigate on my behalf!"

If Simon Templar's self-control had been less than impeccable, his jaw would undoubtedly have dropped as soon as he realised the trend of Patroclos Two's words. But long training had equipped the Saint for an automatic, reflex kind of facial dissemblance which operated in almost any circumstances as the need arose. His jaw therefore on this occasion maintained an unperturbed outline, although beneath the surface air of conversational attention he was gripped by an amazement of such stupendous proportions that it could have sent a hundred jaws plummeting to the centre of the earth.

"You're very shrewd," he said slowly.

"So you confirm it. That you are here to investigate this impostor?"

"I can't deny it," replied the Saint with a faint smile.

"Then it would be ungrateful of me not to accept such an offer. What fee would you ask to find this so-called double and put a stop to his interference in my affairs?"

"Twenty thousand pounds," replied the Saint with a perfectly straight face; and Patroclos Two stood up at once and held out his hand.

"Templar—you're hired."

CHAPTER 6

It was, Simon Templar considered, a situation worthy of inclusion in a cosmic museum of mind-bogglers.

There existed on this earth, indubitably, a billionaire of highly flexible ethics but fabulous efficiency, named Diogenes Patroclos. He was apparently being impersonated with incredible brilliance by an identical double, to the point where his globe-girdling empire was in danger of being smoothly and completely taken over by this perfect imitation of himself. The Saint had now met both the authentic and the spurious Patroclos, and had been hired by both of them to discover and expose the fraud. True, he had not yet collected any down payment on his fees, but that was a minor detail. If he accomplished his job, the real Patroclos could certainly be persuaded to assume the other obligation as one of the incidental expenses of the operation. In fact, if a few more ersatz Patrocloses would turn up, the mission of sorting them out might almost develop into an interesting career.

The only snag was that as of this starting point, the Saint still had to find out who was his real employer and who was the impostor.

However, since there was nothing he could think of for the moment that would hasten a solution of that riddle, he was cheerfully prepared to let it wait and enjoy the liberal dispensations of caviar sandwiches and champagne, whoever was footing the bill for them.

Much later, as the last of the guests were gulping their last stirrup cups, Patroclos Two joined him again and called the footman over.

"Fetch Bainter."

"I . . . I think he's gone to bed, sir."

"Then get him up."

"Yes, sir."

The duplicate mogul turned to Ariadne Two.

"Templar is moving in. Have a room prepared at once."

The girl looked bemused. She glanced from her boss to the Saint and back to her boss again.

"He's moving in tonight?"

"Tonight," asserted Patroclos Two. "Tomorrow you will familiarise him with my itinerary for the next two weeks."

"But, Mr Patroclos—" She broke off, eyeing the Saint with evident mistrust.

"I trust him," said Patroclos Two, as if he had read her thoughts. "As of now, Templar is in full charge of my personal security."

The girl stared at the Saint suspiciously while Patroclos Two moved away to pour himself a cognac; then she quickly left the room.

"Starting next week, Templar, I have a series of vitally important meetings. This impostor will probably try to worm his way into some of them. I want you to—"

"I know, make sure he doesn't horn in and gum up the works."

"Exactly. So that is your immediate assignment. To protect my interests during these meetings. And until the commencement of the meetings, you must accompany me wherever possible, and you must otherwise remain permanently in this house."

"I must *what?*" demanded the Saint.

Patroclos Two took a liberal mouthful of cognac.

"That is the condition fo your employment. I am sure you will see the necessity."

Simon nodded.

"Bottling me up . . . just in case I should decide to get in contact with your other half."

"Nothing personal, you understand." Patroclos Two spread his hands apologetically. "But one cannot be too careful while this double is at large. And once you become separated from me, he could take my place—even convince *you* that he *is* me!"

"And we don't want that, do we?" said Simon with his most Saintly mocking smile. "Has it occurred to you, I wonder, what fun and games we could have if I bumped into the other Patroclos and *he* offered me twenty thousand pounds to remove the impostor—you—from the scene?"

Patroclos Two made an impatient gesture.

"Ha-ha, very amusing, yes. But to me, Templar, this is a serious, a grave matter. My very existence, my identity, is at stake."

"And he—the impostor—is trying to take it over," supplied the Saint. "Right?"

"Just so."

"That's exactly what he'd say about you, if I met him."

There was an apologetic throat-clearing sound beside them, and a small, neat, balding man in a black coat and pin-striped trousers came deferentially forward. Patroclos Two beckoned impatiently, hurrying him closer.

"Bainter, this is Mr Templar. Take a car, go to his home. Pack enough clothes to last two weeks. Bring them back here."

"I'll go with you," Simon added promptly.

"I prefer you to remain here," said Patroclos Two. "I have explained why."

"You also explained a while ago that you trust me with your personal security," Simon pointed out. "You really can't have it both ways. If I go with Bainter here, I'll be under his eye the whole time, and he can report any suspicious behaviour on my part to you afterwards. Anyway, if Bainter tries to open my front door on his own—even with my key—he'll be in for a nasty shock or two. Besides, I prefer to pack my own clothes."

Patroclos Two regarded the Saint for a few moments, and noted the calm determination in his eye.

"All right, Bainter. Bring a car to the door. Mr Templar will go with you."

The valet nodded efficiently and left the room. As soon as he had gone, the Saint said quietly:

"I didn't want to start an argument in front of the servants. I'm going along with your condition of employment, as you called it, because if I'm doing the job it makes sense for me to be here—for the time being. But I shall remain in this house not one minute longer than I choose."

Patroclos Two shrugged.

"As far as I am concerned, you accept the conditions or go. And now I must say goodnight to my last guests. Remember one thing: I am suspicious of everyone. I have not discussed this impostor with any of my staff—not even Ariadne. I expect you to keep your mission just as confidential . . . I will see you in the morning."

Simon nodded. He was still searching for one concrete landmark to give him a bearing on this whole improbable affair; but patches of the all-enveloping fog were beginning to clear. He had done a great deal of almost subconscious groping during the evening, and made a little progress. One obvious question needed to be asked about his brief from Patroclos Two.

"What about the codebook?"

Patroclos Two swung round, and the musketball eyes bulged. "What do you know of the codebook?"

"Only that you keep one," said the Saint easily. "Doesn't it contain some details that are rather crucial in running your businesses? And codes you use to give key instructions to your companies?"

"So . . . ?" Patroclos Two's manner was guarded and suspicious.

"It just occurred to me," the Saint went on, "that this codebook of yours would be a real prize to the impostor, if he chanced to get hold of it."

"Templar, you are absolutely right!" Patroclos Two drummed his fingers together in agitation, and then smashed his fist into the palm of the other hand. "It would be everything he needed. The last step in taking over the life of Diogenes Patroclos. Me! He would be able to control my businesses. I would not be able to cancel his orders . . . The code . . . Templar, the codes must be changed!"

"Have you still got the codebook?" asked the Saint.

"Of course I—" Patroclos Two broke off. "Unless—unless he has already . . . But surely he could not! Even he—" Suddenly his agitation found a focus. "Ariadne!" he snapped at the girl who appeared almost on telepathic cue at his elbow. "Quickly, go to the bedroom safe and fetch my codebook!"

Ariadne Two hurried off, taking a key that Patroclos Two gave her from a bunch he took from his pocket. A minute or two later she returned holding a small black book. Patroclos Two grabbed it from her impatiently and flicked through its pages.

"Thank goodness. The codebook is intact. But tomorrow I will begin work on new codes." He handed the book back to Ariadne. "Put it back in the safe—and return the key to me at once."

Bainter reappeared and said: "I have the car outside, sir."

Simon Templar thought his own thoughts: another patch of mist in the Patroclos landscape was beginning to clear.

CHAPTER 7

"I suppose, Bainter," said the Saint conversationally, "you've been with Mr Patroclos a long time."

"Fourteen years, sir," replied the valet, continuing to unpack and hang up Simon's clothes with deft efficiency.

"You travel with him?"

"No, sir. I just work here."

Simon lounged on the bed and reflected.

"I should think it's quite a problem for a valet, sometimes—keeping track of his employer's changing moods, or tastes."

"I don't quite follow you, sir."

"Well, for example," Simon explained, "just at the moment I'm going through what you might call a discreet-necktie phase. Next month I shall probably get fed up with so much sobriety and break out in jazzed-up jobs that look like chintz chair covers."

Bainter turned from the wardrobe.

"Funny you should say that, sir. Colours, now—well, Mr Patroclos usually wears whatever I lay out for him. A very conservative dresser. But just recently, he brought home some shirts in what I would call quite startling stripes . . ." Bainter tailed off, as if he felt he had been indiscreet.

"Not at all the sort of thing you would approve, Bainter?"

"Well," the valet conceded reluctantly, "I expect I'm a bit old-fashioned. But I think it must have been only a momentary aberration on his part, if I may use the expression. At any rate, the next time he came back from Athens, and I laid out one of those new shirts, he was quite shocked, and asked me where I'd found it."

"He'd forgotten that he bought it himself?"

"It was hardly a shirt that one would forget so quickly."

"Perhaps he was regretting his—aberration—and was trying to save face."

"Possibly, sir. Although Mr Patroclos wouldn't normally be bothered to make that sort of pretence."

Simon could scarcely have hoped for more from the obliging Bainter, who had now finished the unpacking.

"There we are, sir. I trust we haven't forgotten anything."

"Not a thing. We're very efficient, Bainter."

"Thank you, sir . . . I won't keep you, sir. I expect you'll be wanting to get some sleep."

In the doorway the valet turned and added:

"Just one thing, sir. If you should wish to open the window—six inches is the limit, sir. Wider than that, and the alarms start to ring."

"Oh, they do, do they?" said the Saint to himself after Bainter had gone. "We'll see about that."

He undressed and brushed his teeth, but did not change into pyjamas. He lay awake skimming through books from the bedside shelf until three o'clock, when he felt absolutely sure that everyone else in the house would be asleep. Then he got up and dressed again, this time in a sports shirt and slacks, but nothing more. Barefoot, he switched off the light and slipped silently out into the corridor.

It had been easy enough, in the most innocent and casual way, when Bainter was showing him to his room, to learn the exact location of Patroclos's master suite. A pencil flashlight, its bulb masked with a piece of black insulating tape pierced only with a small hole, provided a needle beam of illumination that was all the Saint needed to show him his way.

Patroclos's door was not locked. Simon would have been astonished if it had been, even though he could have easily coped with it—such defensiveness, in the man's own home, would have been almost a symptom of paranoia. And whatever their failings, neither Patroclos had even impressed him as a neurotic type.

In fact, the billionaire—or his impersonator—was snoring with a steady and assertive resonance which proclaimed with every rhythmic decibel the total relaxation and self-confidence of its source.

The Saint moved in like a wraith, guarding even the reduced

ray of his torch from directly touching the huddled shape under the bedclothes. He allowed only enough of a glow to escape from it under his cupped hand to give him bearings, and show him the evening clothes draped over a hanger stand at the foot of the bed; the gold fountain pen, loose change, cigar-clipper, wallet, and diary spread out on the bedside table; and the bunch of keys carelessly dumped among them.

To abstract a bunch of keys from within a yard of the ear of a sleeping man, no matter how profoundly sunk in slumber, without making a single metallic clink that might disturb the sleeper's dreams, requires a skill and steadiness of hand that would dismay any ordinarily adept pickpocket, but Simon Templar accomplished it without any perceptible effect on his pulse rate. Even so, with the keys in his grasp, he stood for long moments as immobile as the Sphinx, watching the recumbent figure in the bed and listening to the regular stertorous breathing, until he was quite sure that his host was not going to be aroused even by an intuitive alarm.

The next problem was to find the safe that the keys fitted. The Saint did not even waste a moment searching for it behind one of the pictures on the walls—that hackneyed hiding place beloved of fiction writers, which on that account must be the first place where any burglar who ever read a book would look. A man as astute as Patroclos would never permit such a crudely obvious installation. The rich wall-to-wall carpet ruled out any trap-door in the floor. The modernistically papered walls precluded the time-honored secret panel, and there was no fireplace to embody some device of dummy bricks.

To Simon Templar, there was no call for random groping and ferreting, which could have been noisy as well as ineffectual. It was, rather, an interesting exercise in applied ratiocination, which could be performed in pensive immobility.

Patroclos Two began threshing about restlessly, as if he might be on the point of waking up; and Simon froze for perhaps thirty seconds until the man in the bed had settled back into apparent slumber.

The direct and logical solution, if there was no reasonable possibility of complicated concealment, would simply be to rely on the sturdiness of the safe itself, and plant it in the handiest place that would be out of the way and out of obtrusive sight. The kind of solution that would be reached in moments by such an exponent of direct action as Diogenes Patroclos.

When the Saint moved, he went straight into the dressing alcove which led off the bedroom, and silently opened the first of the doors of a row of wardrobe closets. And there it was, arrogantly undisguised—a medium-sized but massive steel cube that would have been a major problem to cart away and a total impossibility to break open without considerable uproar.

The Saint had encountered—not to say opened—a good many safes in his time; but in this case he had secured what a purist might have called an unfair advantage. He examined the lock and the bunch of keys in his hand, selected one to try, reached forward . . . and hesitated.

Could the safe be connected to the alarm system? Simon was mentally kicking himself for having neglected to put it out of action before he started on the burglary expedition. But having got that far, it was not in his temperament to turn back. He steeled himself for the jangling of alarm bells, held his breath, and opened the safe.

There was no sound from the machined and well-oiled hinges as the heavy door swung open; and the Saint's long and controlled exhalation of breath that followed was less audible still.

He reached inside the safe and quickly found and extracted the codebook. He flicked through its pages by the fine beam of the pencil torch, only enough to be sure that it was what he wanted, and then in an amazingly short space of seconds he had relocked the safe, shut the wardrobe, put the keys back on Patroclos's bedside table, and crept out as silently as he had arrived.

CHAPTER 8

Back in his own room, the Saint stopped only long enough to seal the codebook in an envelope thoughtfully provided by the secretaire for the convenience of guests who might be seized by an urge to communicate with the outside world, and to pull on his socks. His shoes, for the time being, he preferred to carry, as he found his way down to the ground floor.

Burglar alarms, as a safe general rule, are designed to detect or deter the unwelcome would-be guest who is outside and trying to get in. To anyone who is inside and wanting to get out they constitute only the most minor of nuisances.

Simon stood on a chair to reach the alarm mechanism, which was prominently in view above the front door, and took the simple course of switching it off. Then he replaced the chair and let himself quietly out, leaving the front door on the latch.

The Hirondel was still parked around the corner in Bruton Street, where he had left it the night before. He headed west, and stopped at his mews house to make a phone call to Athens, where he left a brief message. Then he drove on out Cromwell Road, making for the airport.

He was somewhere near Hounslow when his keenly tuned antennae for such matters told him that the big headlights in his rear-view mirror were showing rather more than chance persistence. Few drivers cared to keep pace for long with Simon Templar just for the hell of it; and yet he had no doubt that the same headlights had maintained their position behind him for at least five miles. The Saint had registered their presence from the first; or rather, some idler circuit in his subconscious mind, part of the automatic pilot that was so indispensable to a modern buccaneer, had registered them and had then monitored them moment by moment as he drove until their continued presence began to seem noteworthy, whereupon the appropriate signal had surfaced. Only then did he become conscious of the phenomenon and begin to consider what it might imply.

He slowed abruptly, stepping hard on the brake, and watched in the mirror as the car behind bore down rapidly for a few seconds and then dropped back to its original distance. He speeded up again, and the other car kept pace. And the Saint smiled, hearing the battle trumpets begin to sing in his ears as of old.

Even at its closest the car had been too far behind for him to identify the model. But he guessed that it must be a big car, perhaps a Rolls—or a Bentley.

The Saint's mouth tightened into the fighting lines which had heralded defeat for so many of his adversaries in the past. There were many questions still to be answered, but he knew now with an ice-crisp certainty that there was more to this particular game than he had supposed. The option was there, he knew, to leave it gracefully, but because the Saint was what he was, he knew he could never have done anything but play it out move by move to the final checkmate, or thrust by thrust to the last clash of steel against steel.

He drove on in a mood of fresh thoughtfulness, with the light of battle in his eyes mingling with an amazed conjecture. And before he reached the airport he had laughed aloud, slapped the steering-wheel with both hands, and shaken his head in sheer helpless disbelief.

At the airport he went to the Parnassian Airways desk and handed the sleepy girl on night duty a small manilla envelope addressed FOR THE PERSONAL ATTENTION OF D. PATROCLOS, ATHENS.

"This is very urgent," he stressed. "I've telephoned for it to be collected from Athens Airport."

The girl examined the envelope.

"Of course. Mr Patroclos. A very important man. Our own— our own big boss-man. I will see that it goes by the next plane."

"Thanks. And would you see that your people at the other end notify Mr Patroclos's office as soon as the package arrives there?"

It didn't surprise the Saint to see that the car which had been following was no longer in evidence during the drive back to Patroclos's house in Berkeley Square. He let himself in through the front door, making no particular attempt at silence, and reset the alarm more from neatness than a sense of necessity.

From his room he could see the street at the front of the house; and after a few minutes, as he had expected, a silver Bentley glided to a halt. Out of it stepped Patroclos Two.

Simon heard him enter almost soundlessly by the front door, presumably after somehow disconnecting the alarm from outside. He had only been in view for a few seconds, but that was long enough for Simon to see the confirmation he was looking for.

Patroclos Two was carrying a small manilla envelope.

CHAPTER 9

"What do you mean—how do I know?" snapped Patroclos Two down the telephone. "It is here in the newspaper. What for do I pay you thousands when I can buy a paper for pennies, hah?"

Patroclos Two was surrounded by newspapers, mail, and breakfast things; Ariadne Two sat nearby taking shorthand notes. They both looked up as the Saint, fresh and relaxed but poised for trouble, was ushered in by Bainter the valet.

Ariadne Two nodded a preoccupied greeting. Patroclos Two held the phone receiver briefly aside and bared his teeth in a mechanical smile.

"Good morning, Templar. I trust you slept well. Help yourself from the sideboard. And pour me some more coffee."

And Patroclos Two returned to the phone.

The Saint murmured an equally casual greeting and attended to the coffee. The tycoon or his substitute's manner gave no hint that anything at all untoward had taken place during the night, and for one instant Simon wondered half-seriously if he could have dreamt the entire episode. And yet he knew that it had happened—that he had seen clearly, with his own two eyes, Patroclos Two returning about half past four in the morning with what could only have been the codebook.

Obviously he must have recovered it from the Parnassian Airways girl at the airport—an undertaking that would have been easy enough for the man who, certainly as far as she knew or could tell, was ultimately her employer, and to whom the package was addressed. Simon could well imagine how the scene might have gone: unseen eyes had almost certainly watched as he handed in the envelope; and after that Patroclos Two need only have happened to walk by the Parnassian desk and the girl would be sure to recognise him and mention the package, which he would promptly have claimed there and then, with perhaps a remark to the effect that his presence in London was being kept quiet for business reasons.

Therefore Patroclos Two's strenuous snoring the night before had been as phoney as anything else in this tangle of fakes: he must have been lying awake, fully dressed, waiting for the visit that he guessed the Saint would make. And when Simon left the house, Patroclos Two had followed, taken the car which he had waiting in the square, and settled down on an easy trail.

But why had he chosen, first, to allow the theft of his codebook, next to recover it secretly, and finally to behave as if the whole incident had simply never happened? Simon still had only one answer that would fit, fantastic though it was; and again he went over the reasoning that had led him to it.

If Patroclos Two were the real Patroclos and not the impostor, he would hardly have stood or lain idle while the Saint strolled out with his codebook. Or if he had—perhaps in the hope that the Saint would lead him to the other Patroclos, the impostor—he would certainly have had no need to continue the play-acting once the Saint had parted with the book at the airport. Ergo, this was not the real Patroclos. But on the other hand, if he were the fake, again why should he employ Simon Templar and turn a blind eye to his treachery?

Enjoying his eggs and bacon with an appetite undiminished by such perplexities, the Saint realised that there was a third branch to the maze; and that was the path along which he had travelled some way during the events of the night.

He sipped his coffee reflectively. As a background to his thoughts he had automatically taken in what Patroclos Two was saying on the telephone, and if he had considered it relevant he could easily have recalled every salient point. But now, at the tail-end of the conversation, he switched back to full attention.

"Well, check again! Call me back." Patroclos Two slammed down the phone and made a gesture of despair. "They bleed me, those people. Advance Information Limited. Hah! Should read the limited in front." He turned to Ariadne. "Today you will go over all the schedules with Templar. But first, take a note. Corinthian Tankers . . ."

At a quarter to one, the Saint and Ariadne Two were seated side by side on the sofa in the drawing-room, going over the last of the schedules and notes for Patroclos's meetings. Abruptly Simon stood up and stretched.

"Well, I think that's enough for this morning. It's getting near lunch time. Can we have a drink?"

"Thanks," said Ariadne Two, with perceptibly more warmth in her voice than previously. "That's a cocktail cabinet, over in the corner. I'll have a medium sherry. A large one."

She watched as he poured her drink and mixed himself a dry martini on the rocks. She had begun by mistrusting him, but now she was less sure. About this man with the cavalier smile there was something wildly, untameably adventurous, reckless even, and yet at the same time something innocent and . . . saintly. The word came to her of its own accord, though she knew, from what her boss had told her, that this was the man whom people called the Saint—a man who had known many dangerous adventures across the globe, and who lived always by his own individual, perhaps peculiar, code of justice.

"It's funny," she mused aloud. "Now I know you better it makes even less sense."

Simon handed her a brimming glass of Dry Sack and took an appreciative sip of the cocktail he had poured for himself.

"What does?"

"That you should bluff your way into this house. . . . All that nonsense about knowing me before!"

He eyed her curiously.

"You mean you still don't remember that langouste in Monte Carlo?"

Of course, there had never been any such meeting. But he would have expected an impostor, afraid of being tripped up, to pretend to recall it.

"No, I don't. Look, Mr Templar—"

"Simon," he put in quickly.

"Well—Simon." She looked him straight in the eye, ingenuously. "But I've never even been to Monte Carlo."

The blue eyes widened; they wore their most saintly expression, but in them was a hint of the clear mocking light that the girl had seen before.

"Strange," he said speculatively. "I wonder—could there be *two* Ariadnes?"

The Saint watched her closely as he spoke the line which of all lines must put her acting or her innocence to the test. And the girl looked genuinely puzzled still, seeming not to have taken his remark as seriously meant. She sipped her drink defensively, and had still not answered when the telegram arrived.

They heard the doorbell ring, and the murmur of voices; and then a footman knocked and handed the telegram to Ariadne. She opened and read it, frowned, looked perplexed, read it again, and finally waved away the footman, who was waiting for instructions.

Simon crossed the room and shamelessly read the telegram over her shoulder. It was addressed to Patroclos, and said simply:

INFORMATION RECEIVED STOP PROJECT NOW COMPLETED STOP NO FURTHER ACTION REQUIRED

It was unsigned, but Simon had little doubt that it was intended for him to see. Which was interesting, given that it must be a fake, since he knew that the codebook had never reached Athens.

Ariadne Two shrugged.

"I don't know what it's about. Maybe a secret deal—I don't always travel with him and he doesn't tell me everything."

She took the telegram into the library, where Patroclos Two was busy with work of his own, and the Saint heard phrases of their conversation that drifted through the open door.

"No!" Patroclos Two's voice was raised in anger. ". . . know what the hell it is about? Why couldn't the idiot put his name?"

Then a pause, with Ariadne's voice occasionally murmuring. And then the Saint heard the man say: "Did you show it to Templar? Well, he is my detective for the moment—let him detect."

Ariadne returned looking more puzzled than ever.

"He says he doesn't know whom it is from," she told the Saint with careful grammar. "And he made a joke that you as a clever detective should be able to work it out."

The Saint smiled faintly, knowing that he was beginning to get the measure of the impostor, and that he could see a vaguely forming outline of the last scene in the present act of the elaborate charade that was being played out with himself as one of the principals—and with Ariadne Two, in all probability, as another.

That is, unless he introduced some twist of his own into the script. And one of Simon Templar's special forms of mischief was refusing to go too far along with the most studiously prepared scenario, and introducing disconcerting variations of his own.

In this case, it was an impulsive decision that somewhere along the line he had to pick someone who was not a fraud but a dupe, lay some cards on the table, and make an ally. On what could only have been a psychic hunch, based at best on somewhat longer acquaintance, he decided that the time had come to bet on Ariadne Two.

Perhaps it was a reckless gamble; but if the Saint had never taken a chance he would never have taken anything.

He took another fortifying pull at his martini, as some stalwart soul on the bank of a frozen lake might brace himself for the shock, and took the plunge.

"Ariadne," he said quietly, "has it occurred to you that your boss could be a fake?"

She looked at him blankly.

"*What?*"

"Your boss has employed me to winkle out an impostor who looks exactly like him and who's been taking his place here, there, and everywhere. But I've reason to believe that *he's* the impostor himself."

Simon waited while his words sank in; and the girl, as he had expected, looked at him as if at a lunatic child who had just asserted that the moon was made entirely of peanut butter.

"I expect you know the ancient Greek legend of the Minotaur," he went on soothingly. "This was a monster, half man and half bull, who lived in a maze of caves in Crete, and lived by gobbling up human sacrifices who were sent in to feed him. One of these was eventually a bloke named Theseus, who just happened to have made it with the daughter of the king. When his turn came, she gave him a spool of thread to reel out behind him. Theseus

killed the Minotaur, and found his way out of the labyrinth by
following the thread back. You were named after her—Ariadne.
Now, you could help me find my way out of this crazy maze."

"But that's quite ridiculous!" she exclaimed as soon as she had
found her voice. "Mr Patroclos—an impostor? Do you think I
don't know him after five years?"

"Believe me, this is no ordinary impostor." The Saint's cool
voice sounded so reasonable that she was compelled almost
against her will to give it a hearing. "This, even though I doubted
the propositon myself, is what might justifiably be called the perfect impostor. The copy and the original are very nearly impossible to tell apart. And I know," he added. "I've seen them both."

"But it's unbelievable. How could—"

The girl's next words were masked by a ferocious bull-like bellow from the library, and they heard Patroclos Two screaming
down the telephone.

"Impossible! Quite impossible! I tell you, I sent no such message!"

Simon followed Ariadne into the library. Patroclos Two was in
an almost uncontrollable rage, thumping a fist on the desk in time
with his words.

"I don't care! Check again. . . . Then double check, you
fool! . . . Of course I'll countermand it. Just as soon as I can
make out a coded message. Do it then. Ring me back—and
hurry!"

Patroclos Two's eyes blazed and he slammed down the phone.
"Ariadne—upstairs, the safe. Get my codebook."

He threw her the bunch of keys from his pocket, and she hurried off. Patroclos Two paced back and forth with a ferociously in-
dignant expression on his face.

"Why? *Why?*"

"What's happened?" asked the Saint calmly.

"Six cargo ships—on their way to Singapore. In mid-ocean, suddenly they change course, for an unknown destination. Unknown
to *me*. Who ordered it? The Communications Office say I did—
from *Athens. Me!* But I am here!"

The Saint went very still.

"Then it's obvious, isn't it," he said quietly, "that the *other* you is *there*."

Patroclos Two stared at him.

"No, no. . . . Even he . . ." He seemed to consider for a moment. "Without my personal code—"

"What are these ships carrying?" the Saint interrupted, ignoring Patroclos Two's mention of the codebook.

"Who cares what they are carrying?"

"It seems *he* does."

"Oh—agricultural machinery . . . a little paint, fertilisers . . . Ariadne burst in, breathless.

"The codebook—it isn't there, sir."

"Of course it's there," said Patroclos impatiently. "You returned it to the safe yourself only yesterday."

Ariadne looked almost guilty.

"But it's not there now. I checked thoroughly."

He stared at her, eyes blazing again, then grabbed the keys from her hand and strode from the room. Simon shook his head, chuckling.

"Tremendous act your boss puts on. You should try and persuade him to go on the stage. Put it to him that he owes it to the world. As it is, he's denying the theatre public so much fabulous talent."

"But this is serious! If the codebook is missing—and I *did* put it back—"

She rushed out in Patroclos Two's wake still almost visible, and the Saint followed. They found him in the bedroom raking all the papers out of the safe and onto the floor of the wardrobe. He glared around as they came into the room; and then he turned on the Saint, and there were little red specks of anger burning in the cores of his eyes.

"You!" he shouted, stabbing a sudden accusing finger. "You took the codebook! That cable from Athens—"

The Saint clapped politely.

"Bravo. Beautiful lines, beautifully delivered."

"You're working for the other side!"

Ariadne looked helplessly from one man to the other: from the squat powerful figure of Diogenes Patroclos (or was it his dou-

ble?), with his musketball eyes and livid expression, to Simon
Templar, calm and smiling and insolent. And the Saint's voice
floated coolly across the room with a challenge that was dazzlingly
simple and which he knew Patroclos Two would be unable to re-
fuse with credibility.

"Whether I'm working for him or not," he pointed out, "it
seems clear that the other Patroclos is in Athens. Why aren't we
there, knocking hell out of him?"

And in the pause that followed, he could almost hear the whir-
ring of gears in Patroclos Two's brain, as the mogul considered
the implications of that logical proposal. For perhaps a minute he
stood silent, with his head tilted slightly to one side as if to give
him a new perspective on the Saint; and then he nodded thoughtfully.

"Of course, Templar. As I should have expected, you are absolutely right." He turned briskly to Ariadne. "How soon can my
plane be ready?"

"It was having an engine overhaul, you remember. It was supposed to be finished tomorrow."

"Well, contact the pilot at once. They will have to work over-
time and finish tonight. We will face this confounded impostor
first thing tomorrow. Pack your bags. And cancel all my appoint-
ments. Nothing is as important as this!"

CHAPTER 10

Patroclos's private plane was faster than the aircraft in commercial service, and it landed in Athens, after a refuelling stop in Milan, only eight hours after leaving London. It was almost nine o'clock in the morning there.

"Our arrival at the office must be a complete surprise," said Patroclos Two as he hailed a taxi outside the airport. "Obviously we cannot afford to alert the impostor and give him a chance to escape."

Simon Templar raised an eyebrow.

"And what do you propose to do if by some chance he isn't there?"

"We must follow!" Patroclos Two's tone was vehement. "Wherever he goes, we will follow. Now that we have begun, now that we are on his trail, his man *must* be finally tracked down and confronted!"

"And of course," added the Saint wearily, "you'll be wanting to get your codeback before you arrange to have this double of yours chucked into the sea. *If* he has it, that is."

Patroclos Two's face was expressionless.

"And you, Templar. If I find that my suspicions are justified—that you have been working for *him* as well as me . . . well, I will have to decide what to do when the time comes. But you should know that Diogenes Patroclos is never double-crossed with impunity!"

Ariadne Two seemed totally confused by recent events, and had said practically nothing during the flight. The Saint supposed that she was doing some hard thinking of her own. She appeared to have been genuinely surprised when he had told her about the Patroclos double; and he had little doubt that before long she would receive several further jolts to her system.

When they reached the headquarters office building, Patroclos Two strode straight through the entrance and along the corridor to his own office suite, with the Saint and the girl following close behind.

As they burst into the outer office, Ariadne One looked up from her desk with a startled expression. Ariadne Two gasped at the sight of the girl who was almost her double—although the resemblance, when Simon saw them together, was not nearly so uncannily identical as that of Patroclos One and Two.

The Saint nudged her.

"See what I mean? Two Ariadnes."

And Ariadne One looked equally bemused.

"Mr Patroclos—" she began.

"Who the hell are you?" he snapped, and flung open the big double doors to the inner office.

The room was empty; and Patroclos Two turned in a fury as savage as the one that had gripped him in London.

"Where is he? This man who looks like me?"

"Who, Mr Patroclos?" Ariadne One seemed uncomprehending. "Did you . . . forget something?"

"Remember me, Ariadne?" said the Saint; and the girl looked relieved and grateful for the intervention.

"Mr Templar. Yes, of course."

"Well, this is the *other* Patroclos."

"You are supposed to be *Ariadne*?" queried Patroclos Two.

"But of course I am Ariadne," said the girl slowly, looking in amazement first at Patroclos Two and then at her own double.

"Don't try to work it out," advised the Saint. "Just tell us where he is."

"But you . . . I mean he . . . well, you just left, Mr Patroclos."

"How long ago?" asked Simon quickly.

"Just two minutes."

"Where's he going?"

"He didn't say. He got a phone call."

"Where from?" barked Patroclos Two.

The girl looked uncomfortable under the double-barrelled cross-examination.

"From the airport. He collected his briefcase—and rushed out."

"How come we didn't pass him on our way in here?" asked the Saint.

"He went out the back way to the car."

Simon crossed swiftly to one of the windows; and then he uttered *sotto voce* a fluent string of extremely unsaintly observations as he saw the purple Rolls disappearing from the parking lot behind the building.

"Come on!" called the Saint, rushing for the door. "Let's get after him. The airport's a safe bet. Ariadne One"—and he pointed at the girl to leave her in no doubt as to which of them was meant —"get us a car at the front—*gregora!*"

Patroclos Two told the driver, in Greek, to go like the wind; and the resulting ride lived even in the Saint's memory for years afterwards. But when they arrived at the airport Patroclos's plane in which they had recently flown from London was just taking off, and the purple Rolls was being driven back off the runway.

Patroclos Two shook his fist in impotent rage at the dwindling aircraft.

"Now you believe who is real?" he demanded, stabbing the air with his finger. "*I* arrive—*he* runs!"

"You do seem to be ahead on points," Simon admitted. "But it's still anybody's game."

Suddenly Patroclos flicked his fingers.

"Of course. The police. They must warn Interpol. Wherever he lands he must be caught!"

"We needn't trouble Interpol," said the Saint.

Patroclos Two looked impatient.

"So? What is your suggestion?"

"That plane was practically out of gas when we got here. It's hardly had time to refuel."

Patroclos Two's eyes widened with realisation.

"You mean—he cannot be going far?"

"It should be easy to check on whatever other airports there are within range," said the Saint. "Probably he would have to land somewhere in Greece—or else he crashes!"

CHAPTER 11

"Look," expostulated Ariadne One, "for the fourth time, all I know is that I work for Diogenes Patroclos—*the* Patroclos. He *must* be genuine."

"She's lying," said Ariadne Two tersely.

"I'm not!" Ariadne One protested indignantly.

"Then why pretend to be me?"

"Why should I pretend to be you?"

"What's your full name?"

"Ariadne Kyriakides."

"*I'm* Ariadne Kyriakides."

"You're lying!"

"Girls, girls!" the Saint interrupted. "Now, Ariadne One—that's you—how long have you been working for the man you know as Patroclos?"

"Five years."

"Ariadne Two?"

"Five years."

"Well, the fake can't have been going that long," said the Saint slowly. "So one of you *must* be lying. Can either of you prove you've been working for him that long?"

Ariadne One replied at once.

"Yes. You can check with the Bannerman Bureau in London."

"But *I* was employed through Bannerman's!" put in Ariadne Two indignantly.

The Saint sighed.

"So unless Bannerman's carry photos of the girls they find work for—which they won't—we're up against a brick wall."

The telephone in Patroclos's outer office, where the three were talking, rang at that moment, and Ariadne One answered it.

"Yes. . . . This is Mr Patroclos's personal secretary. . . . Yes." As she listened, her eyes widened with horror. "Yes, I will tell him."

She put down the phone and turned.

"The plane crashed. Into the sea, near Andros—"

She was on her way to the inner office, where Patroclos Two had been rooting through papers left by his other half, but he met her at the door.

"I heard that," he said. "Did anyone survive?"

"The plane was smashed to pieces and sank at once. They say that no one could have been alive."

"And they may never even find a body," Patroclos said. "It would have been interesting to see this man who looked so much like me. That telephone call just before he left—he must have had an accomplice at the airport who warned him when we arrived."

Patroclos had a grim expression which boded ill for the traitor when he was discovered. He looked at the Saint. "So . . . it is over."

Ariadne One gave a sudden choking cry and slumped down at the desk, burying her face in her arms. After a while she looked up, red-eyed.

"I had to go on pretending," she said with unsteady quiet in her voice, "while there was still hope."

"Then *he* was the fake?" said Ariadne Two.

"Yes." She nodded sadly. "I didn't know at first. I . . . I've only been with him a year, but he had been playing the part for some while before that. Then he offered me a lot of money to play along . . . and he persuaded me to change my name."

"And do you realise," snapped Patroclos, "what trouble you have caused me?"

"I . . . I'm sorry, Mr Patroclos. But you see, *he* was my boss. He was the man who employed me, and my loyalty was to him. And when he took me on, I thought he *was* you . . ."

Patroclos looked at the Saint.

"Satisfied, Templar?"

"Hm, well, there are still a couple of things I don't understand."

"Then we'll discuss them later. Also your own position—even

your fee. Yes, Templar, I think I understand the position in which
you found yourself. You were working for him first, yes? You
believed that he was the real Patroclos. And then *I* employed
you. So, it was difficult for you. Whom to trust? But you have
done what I asked. You have played your part in ridding me of
this nuisance. So we will talk later. For the moment, this young
lady and I"—he indicated Ariadne One—"are going to the police!"

Ariadne One flinched.

"Oh no, please . . ."

Patroclos spread his hands reassuringly.

"Your position too was difficult. I will not make any charges.
But you must give a full statement of all this. I must dissociate
myself from the damage this man has done."

"You don't waste a second, do you?" said the Saint. "You're the
real Patroclos all right."

Patroclos smiled.

"We will see you presently," he said, taking Ariadne One by the
arm and steering her out.

Ariadne Two—who after all was the real Ariadne—still looking
bemused, watched them go.

"Well, that's that."

"Is it?" asked the Saint, with that bantering lift to the eyebrows
that she had come to know.

"Well . . ." The girl hesitated. "Well, isn't it?"

"End of story? Everything neatly wrapped up and explained?
Not in my book, sweetheart. Not by a long way." Simon had
begun searching through the desk drawers, tossing papers out and
carelessly stuffing them back. "What about the pilot?"

"He was killed with the impostor."

"But he must have known that the plane was low on fuel. After
all, he'd just flown it here from London. So why did he take off?"

"Maybe he was forced to?"

The Saint shook his head.

"Fly a plane at gunpoint—to almost certain death? No, I don't
think so. And there's something else."

"What?"

Simon slid a filing cabinet drawer shut with a thud.

"The codebook. It never left London."

"It never left? But I don't understand. We couldn't find it when we looked . . ." Ariadne stared at him.

"Oh, I took it out of the safe all right," the Saint explained. "I got it as far as the airport. *Your* Patroclos picked it up."

She followed him as he moved to the inner office.

"So if the codebook didn't reach Athens, the ships—"

"Couldn't have been diverted from here," supplied the Saint. "Right. Your Patroclos must have done the diverting from London. *He* had the book all the time. You see, it just doesn't fit. And it's too pat—plane crashes, impostor killed, case solved. And," the Saint added softly, "Templar forgiven."

The girl digested the implications in silence for a few minutes, watching him systematically rifle Patroclos's big mahogany desk.

"What are you looking for?" she asked.

"Cargo manifests, showing what's on those ships."

Ariadne opened a filing cabinet and started to shuffle through papers; and she didn't see the Saint's brows angle together in interest at what he had found in the bottom drawer of the desk. A Dictaphone fitted snugly into the drawer—loaded, with a record ready to play.

There was an earphone lying in the drawer; Simon plugged it in, held it loosely up to one ear, and switched the machine on. He listened thoughtfully to the harsh voice of Diogenes Patroclos.

It said: "*Templar—I am told you have seen the impostor. Why are you wasting time telephoning instead of watching him? . . . I am here in Athens. If you have seen the impostor, it should make your job easier. Please do not waste my time telling me that I am being impersonated. That I already know. Goodbye.*"

Simon reversed the machine, restarted it, and held out the earphone to Ariadne. She listened with a blank expression.

"Does Dio always record his own telephone conversations?" he asked.

"I never knew about it. Perhaps he wanted a record sometimes, for his own protection, or something."

"Or something," agreed the Saint.

Ariadne continued going through the files, and suddenly pulled out a folder.

"Here, will this help? Papers on a ship called the *Macedonian*

Queen. She was supposed to sail for Singapore with the other five but she was held up with steering trouble . . . There's a repair bill. But she's still here."

"In Athens?" The Saint could hardly believe his luck.

"In Piraeus, the port. But she sails at midnight."

"Ariadne," said the Saint, "I love you. Call me Theseus."

CHAPTER 12

The *Macedonian Queen* was not hard to find among the few freighters berthed in Piraeus at the time. Simon Templar and the girl simply wandered along the wharf to which she guided him until they came to the smart-looking but unexceptional freighter painted in the blue and gold Patroclos colours. The gangplank was unguarded, and only one seaman was visible on deck, a Greek in a grubby dark-blue sweat-shirt and dungarees who was leaning over the rail at the bow, with his back to them. It seemed quite probable that he represented the entire watch left on board, while the rest of the crew were enjoying their last hours ashore.

Patroclos had still not returned to the office by one o'clock, when the Saint had insisted on taking Ariadne out for an *ouzo*, leaving a note for him, and then to lunch.

"There's nothing in my contract that says I have to go without regular meals," he maintained, "and I'm sure there isn't in yours either."

They had eaten *dolmades* and *moussaka*, but he had declined to be tempted by *retsina*, the traditional resin-flavored wine which is said to have been invented by the Greeks to discourage hostile invaders from swilling or swiping it. Simon found it just as unpalatable as the earlier barbarians, and ordered a bottle of Cypriot Othello instead.

He had sensed that while Ariadne might not yet be a full ally, she would not be an enemy, and decided at the end of the meal to tell her his plan.

"I want to have a look around the *Macedonian Queen*. I think I might find the answers to some of the questions that are still nagging me. But I'm not going to tell Dio."

"But he'll expect you to be in the office if he wants you," she objected.

"The impostor has crashed. Technically, my job is finished. I'm free to slope off and go sight-seeing if I feel like it. How do I get to Piraeus?"

She pondered for only a few seconds.

"I'll take you."

"But you've still got a job to keep."

"And I've got more questions, too. I shall telephone the office and leave a message that everything this morning has given me such a terrible headache that I have to go home and go to bed, and I will be back tomorrow."

That was how they came to be lurking behind a pile of crates near the untended gangway in the gathering dusk, unnoticed by the bored seaman on so-called "watch" on the foredeck. The Saint gripped the girl's arm gently.

"This is where I go aboard; and it could develop into a rough party if they catch me. Stay out of sight and keep your fingers crossed!"

"I'm going with you," said Ariadne in a determined voice, "since I brought you as far as this."

The Saint smiled at her and stood up.

They glided unobserved up the narrow gangplank onto the deck, and then down a ladder through a hatchway into the after cargo hold. The lighting was dim, but they could see to move among the mountains of crates, in several shapes and sizes, that were stacked there. Simon peered at random at the export labels, bringing his pencil flashlight to bear on them and spoke in a whisper.

"As you'd expect. All Singapore. That's where the ships were officially headed."

"This label says Paint. Why don't we have a look inside?" suggested the girl in an equally low voice.

Lying on one of the crates was a pair of metal-shears and a crowbar. There was a sharp twang as Simon used the shears to sever the steel customs bond on the crate, and for a minute or more they both froze in silence, listening for the sound of approaching footsteps. Then gingerly, and with one ear still cocked, the Saint prised up the lid a few inches and peered into the crate.

"What's inside?" asked the girl.

"Paint," said Simon pressing the lid back on. "Let's try this long one marked Agricultural Implements."

He repeated the breath-bating procedure with the shears and crowbar. The lid lifted more easily, and inside they saw dozens of gleaming hoes. But the Saint, carelessly for him, rammed the lid back on with unnecessary force and more than the unavoidable minimum of noise, and a hinged side of the crate dropped down. Inside, in a compartment beneath the hoes, were revealed at least a score of carbines.

The Saint gave a low whistle.

"A few hoes on top, and a rich harvest of guns underneath! And they're the very latest thing. And American! But the interesting question is, Where are they going?"

The girl reached into one end of the gun compartment and took out a folded piece of paper.

"Look. Some kind of instruction leaflet. With diagrams. But it's printed in Chinese."

Simon took the paper from her and studied it, frowning.

"Not Chinese . . . My knowledge of oriental scripts isn't all it might be," he confessed. "But I'm pretty sure I've seen something like this before. It's like ancient Sanskrit characters, only there's a difference in the way they're arranged on the page." He spread out the paper on a crate in front of her. "Look—if you turn it so that the diagrams are the right way up, you can see which way the text goes. See—it's in vertical lines—like Chinese. Sanskrit characters, Chinese arrangement. And the only script I know of like that is Korean! So that's the game!"

"The guns are going to Korea?"

"North Korea," said the Saint quietly. "American weapons, being exported for use against the Americans themselves in the war. And, of course, against the South Koreans."

"Couldn't they be going to the South?"

He shook his head.

"There'd be no reason to hide them if they were. No, this little lot's bound for North Korea all right, you could bet your life on that. And so are those other five ships, no doubt. Mystery solved."

He paused thoughtfully and then added: "But not the immediate problem."

"What is that?"

"How to stop this shipment."

"We will tell Mr Patroclos, and he will tell the police."

"There's no law against exporting arms. And the crew would swear that they knew nothing about it, anyhow—whether they did or not. Besides, there are the five ships that've already sailed. They've got to be stopped."

"Mr Patroclos could radio them and order them to turn back."

"*Could*—but would he?" Simon's expression was sardonic. "Dio may not be as unscrupulous as some people say he is, but I never heard of him having a reputation as a great philanthropist. Having those ships turned back and unloaded now, and maybe tied up for months in some official investigation, would cost him a small fortune in overheads and lost time and freights. No, I'm afraid that with his impostor disposed of he'd be liable to think it more practical to just let this operation take its course."

Ariadne looked troubled and uncertain.

"Those other five ships have got to be intercepted, by force if necessary." The Saint was frowning as he virtually went on thinking aloud. "But that's a major naval operation, and nobody's going to launch it just on our say-so. Someone pretty big has got to verify what we've seen here. Like, someone from the American Embassy."

He gripped the girl suddenly by the shoulders.

"Ariadne, will you help me?"

"How?"

"Go and phone the Ambassador. Say it's a red-alert United Nations emergency. Give my name. It may not shine like a bishop's, but I think it's got enough clout to make him listen. Have him send someone responsibile down here, preferably his naval attaché, at flank speed. You meet him, and bring him aboard."

She stared up at him searchingly, hesitating, and finally nodded.

"Yes, I will do it. But what about you?"

He smiled a reckless smile, and the blue eyes danced.

"I'll stay here and make sure, somehow, that they don't sail before he gets here. Also, my curiosity's killing me, and I want to see what other little surprises they've got stashed away in these boxes."

He climbed to the top of the hatchway stepladder, peered cautiously over the coaming and around the deck, and was back almost instantly, dropping lightly to the floor.

"All clear," he whispered; and then he gripped her shoulders lightly again and kissed her on the cheek. "Good luck, Ariadne."

"And you . . . Simon. And when Mr Patroclos finds out what I have done, I hope you can find me another job."

Then she was gone.

And the Saint soon became so absorbed in his discoveries that he failed altogether to notice that a pair of dark eyes had begun to watch him from the hatchway above.

It was only when three burly Greek seamen had already begun to descend the stepladder that the slight scuffing sound of their bare feet alerted him, and he whirled around just in time to see the first one launching himself off the ladder towards him.

In the circumstances it was a reasonably promising move on the seaman's part, since any ordinary man would have reacted too slowly to avoid the approximately two hundred pounds of foot-first Greek that hurtled towards Simon Templar's head. But the Saint was no ordinary man; which was unfortunate for the Greek seaman, who like many before him could never afterwards fully fathom how it was that when he reached the area of space occupied by his target, there was nothing but emptiness where Simon Templar ought by all ordinary laws to have been. The sailor's heels hit the side of one crate, splitting it open and shunting it a couple of feet along the floor of the hold; and the crate that was stacked on top of it lost just enough of its support to topple over onto the man's prone body before he could move. There was a sharp painful *oomph* as the breath was knocked out of him and what sounded like the cracking of a few ribs.

Simon ducked behind a taller pile of crates, and waited with every nerve fibre taut like piano wire as the other two seamen dropped off the ladder and began cautiously circling towards him from opposite directions. One of them shouted loudly in Greek, presumably to summon reinforcements; and then suddenly he began a rush. But the Saint toppled a crate over in his path, and then whirled to face the other man's charge. He took a heavy but clumsy blow to the chest, and countered with a long hard straight left which he planted with immediately visible effect square in the centre of the seaman's already bulbous nose. The man sat down hard on his tailbone, clutching his injured proboscis with tender fingers through which a stream of blood instantly began to flow.

Meanwhile his shipmate had scrambled around the obstructing crate, and threw himself onto Simon's back. But to Simon's judo training this was about as effective as a novice equestrian leaping onto the back of a skittish bronco, and the man found himself sailing through the air onto the top of a crate.

"Stop, you fools! It's Templar!" Suddenly the voice of Diogenes Patroclos cut raspingly across the hold. "He works for me. Stop it!"

The crewmen pulled themselves awkwardly together and backed sullenly off as Patroclos and another man in the uniform of a ship's captain descended the ladder.

"Well, if it isn't good old Dio Two—or is it One?" murmured the Saint. "Do you realise that you're breaking up the best workout I've had for about four days?"

"Templar, I'm sorry. Those idiots didn't realise—"

"They realised, all right. Just look around."

Simon indicated the open crates, then casually reached inside one, took out a rifle, and threw it down with a clatter at Patroclos's feet.

Patroclos seemed utterly astonished. He picked up the rifle and examined it, peered into the open cases, and then turned to the ship's Captain.

"What is the meaning of this?" he snapped.

The Captain shrugged sullenly and said nothing. Simon rested one foot on a crate, folded his arms, and slowly shook his head in wonderment. And he laughed.

"I'll be happy to explain on the Captain's behalf, Dio," he began. "Singapore was just a paper destination—to satisfy the authorities. All that nonsense about the ships being diverted! They weren't diverted at all. From the outset they were bound for North Korea."

Patroclos swore fluently in Greek.

"American arms for North Korea . . . ? If this is true, then it must be that impostor who—"

"There is no impostor," said the Saint coolly. "And there never has been. You manufactured him. It was you all the time."

CHAPTER 13

In the ensuing silence all the muscles of Patroclos's face and neck seemed to be working; the black musketball eyes burned with anger; and for the first time, the shadow of something like fear flitted across the strong swarthy face. Patroclos flicked a nervous tongue over his lips, which had suddenly turned pale. At last he found his voice.

"Then why would I hire you?" he demanded harshly.

"You needed an impartial witness to prove that this other man —this scapegoat-to-be—existed."

"Which you are."

"I might have been," Simon conceded. "I'll admit you had me flummoxed at first. Your planning was tremendous—and your psychology was pretty good too . . . The girl at the airport . . . The heavies at the hotel to warn me off—you knew that was the one sure way to get me on the hook . . . The quick dash to London— in your private plane you were probably there before I was . . . The slightly altered appearance and voice . . . The briefing of your staff at this end . . . The invented detail—"

"And how did I make you come to Athens in the first place?" Patroclos scoffed.

"You didn't. That was sheer opportunism. Oh, you'd planned to set someone up before long, of course—I just happened along at the ideal time. I haven't always been an upright citizen, but I do have a reputation, though I say so myself, for being nobody's patsy, and I daresay the challenge appealed to your vanity. If you could fool me—and you very nearly did—you could fool anybody. Anyhow, you seized the chance when you saw my name in a passenger list. And then you exploited it for all it was worth."

"You are beginning to sound like some kind of lunatic."

"You played me like a fish on a line. For a long time, I had an uneasy feeling I was being manipulated, but I couldn't quite see how. But that's your forte—manipulation. Dio, there's no doubt the plan was brilliant. There was just one serious flaw. . . ."

Diogenes Patroclos stared at him impassively.

"Which was . . . ?"

"The whole basic premise," continued the Saint. "As I said right at the start, the idea of a perfect impersonation is a lot of baloney."

"And yet that impostor has still deceived you," Patroclos persisted. "You saw with your own eyes—"

"—just what you meant me to see," Simon completed with inexorable calm. "You did it so well you almost had me believing in this darned impersonator—and to begin with I was about as sceptical as anyone could be. Appearance, voice, mannerisms, knowledge, habits—a human being's just too complicated a thing to be mimicked that closely. My whole instinct was against it. But I'll admit you played your hand cleverly enough to get me seriously wondering if I could have been wrong after all. Starting when I saw you and the other Ariadne in London."

"But I suppose I was sure that you *would* see us?" Patroclos argued sarcastically.

"You'd given me the address as a starting point. You knew I'd go there and watch the house—and before long I'd be bound to see you. And you guessed that as soon as I did, the first thing I'd do would be to check by phoning Athens and asking to speak to you there. You even had something pretty good worked out for that. A simple trick, but good enough."

"What was that?"

"A Dictaphone recording for your Ariadne here to turn on, with the kind of answer that would be sure to fit in well enough with the kind of thing I could be expected to say."

"You should be writing detective stories," Patroclos said, but his confidence was beginning to have a hollow ring.

"My friend Charteris has often said the same thing," Simon agreed good-humouredly. "I must have a go at it one day. But when I do, I'll have to give you credit for some beautiful touches, like for instance pretending some time back to have forgotten about some startling shirts you'd ordered before your last trip away. You figured I'd be sure to find an opportunity to question Bainter—as I did."

Diogenes Patroclos was no quitter. His innumerable worst enemies had never said that of him, and it would have been a ludicrous assertion in any case. A man who gives up before the ultimate sanction simply does not get into the billionaire bracket. Even now, Simon felt, in allowing the argument to go on to the almost absurd lengths of the time-honoured detective-story cliché in which the stereotype sleuth spends endless minutes of the last act explaining with clairvoyant precision just what everybody else was plotting and pretending, Patroclos was in fact treating himself to a complete preview of the case against himself, probing it for any weak points, and assessing every possibility of brazening out his own defence.

"If you had been clever enough to catch that impostor," Patroclos said, "his confession would have proved what nonsense you are talking. But now I think you are only making these absurd accusations to cover up your own failure."

"Yes, that was a grand finale," mused the Saint. "The dash after your Rolls with no one in it but the driver—and the plane with no one but the pilot. I suppose he did parachute out while the plane was still over land, after setting the automatic pilot to make it crash in the sea? Or was there a time bomb in the briefcase that went on board . . . ? Anyhow, conveniently complete end of impersonator, leaving it theoretically impossible to prove that he never existed. Except that you're still stuck at least with one accomplice too many."

"Who?"

"That chauffeur, who knows that no double of yours got on the plane. And whatever you're paying him, or unless you've already disposed of him, I bet he'll talk under pressure. And the pressure will certainly be applied when I tell my story, and back it up with that Dictaphone record which you so carelessly didn't erase."

The Saint's remorseless prosecution came to this conclusion with such relaxed assurance that he might have commanded three times the muscle of Patroclos's minions, instead of being in a

lonely minority of one. And the shipping Midas, could only have
known that the last hope of bluff and bluster was gone.

"You can't win 'em all," Simon told him. "Give up, Dio."

Patroclos scowled at him for a long moment.

"So," he said finally. "So much work for nothing . . . But if
you will not be a witness *for* me"—he spat out the words—"you
will never be one *against* me!"

He turned to the Captain, who obviously spoke little if any
English, and who had been listening uncomprehendingly to this
lengthy dialog while his crewmen waited for a lead from him.

"Kill him!" he commanded, in Greek. "*Skotoseton!*"

And the Captain pulled a revolver from his hip pocket, showing
only relief at receiving such a simple order.

But the Saint had long foreseen how desperate his situation
might become, and had resolved that if he was destined to end his
career down in that cargo hold, trapped like a rat behind a pile of
boxes, it would only be after he had given the ungodly a show for
their money; after he had gathered up and released every last mil-
ligram of furious fighting energy that was to be found in his body.

Every dyne of alertness and determination went into gauging
the arrival of that moment and responding to it with almost su-
pernatural speed so as to avoid the deadly lump of lead that would
hurtle out of the gun barrel that was swinging up towards him in
the Captain's hand. And in the fraction of a second before the
Captain completed his pressure on the trigger, the Saint dived
sideways; and the bullet sang past his left ear and thudded into a
crate.

Overlaid on the loud reverberations he heard Patroclos shout:
"Fool! Be careful! The ammunition!"

And then in what seemed like a mere fluent continuation of
that dive, the Saint swept up the metal-shears he had been using
with his right hand and hurled them at the Captain. They
smashed point first into the Captain's right arm, and he dropped
the gun with a yelp. Before any of the seamen could reach him
the Saint had snatched up a grenade from one of the broken
crates.

He held it aloft in both hands, and there was cold steel in his
voice as he spoke.

"If anyone makes a move, I'll pull out the pin and throw this pineapple without the slightest hesitation. This whole lot'll go up with a bang—and all of you with it."

Patroclos and the Captain and crew froze. The Saint began to edge towards the ladder.

"Don't look so worried, Dio," he mocked. "I'm sure you can buy enough sympathy from the Greek authorities to stay out of serious trouble. Of course, you'll never be *persona grata* in America again, but there are still other continents for you to operate in. Any of them must be better than being scattered around Piraeus in small pieces."

"Wait!" Patroclos said hoarsely. "Let us not be hasty. Why can we not come to an arrangement?"

The Saint shook his head.

"No dice," he said. "You may find it hard to believe, but I've still got a few silly old-fashioned principles propping up my halo. I'm just not on the side of the Commies, even when they call themselves North Koreans, and nothing you can offer would persuade me to help them.

He had almost reached the foot of the ladder, his glance constantly shifting from one man to another, alert for the slightest hint of a hostile move. If he had to, he was prepared in the last resort to use the grenade . . . But only if it positively was the very last resort.

Out of the corner of an eye he saw Patroclos crawling on all fours between two crates towards the Captain's revolver where it had fallen.

Simon leapt across the intervening space and got one foot on the gun just as the mogul, his face a mask of vengeful fury, snatched at it. Then the Saint stooped down to grasp the butt, and jerked it savagely. Patroclos kept his grip, and the gun came up off the floor; somehow in the struggle, the gun went off, and Diogenes Patroclos crumpled and rolled slackly over with a bright red stain slowly spreading across his white linen shirt-front.

Simon straightened up, with the revolver now reinforcing the menace of the grenade he still held in his other hand.

"Anyone else want to try his luck?" he inquired grimly. There were no takers.

CHAPTER 14

Simon Templar refilled Ariadne's glass and his own from the *ouzo* bottle, and put his feet on the desk.

"It was about the nearest thing you could have to a perfect impersonation. An amazing idea, if you think about it—a man impersonating himself. What a show! And I was the leading player—in the audience!"

The Patroclos empire was in disarray and confusion; with the consent of the Greek government the American Navy, acting for the United Nations, had intercepted the other five ships and seized all the cargoes. Simon was resigned to staying around for a few days longer in Athens to make further statements to the police; Ariadne was similarly resigned to helping to sort out the loose ends in the office; and both had made up their minds to enjoy the enforced stay.

"That poor girl," mused Ariadne. "He was her boss, and she stayed loyal to him. I feel sorry for her."

"So do I," agreed the Saint. "He exploited her as he exploited everyone else. She played her part magnificently, right down to the tears when the news of the plane crash came in."

The girl toyed with her glass reflectively. It was not the first time, nor would it be the last, that they had shared a need to recapitulate and review some of the complications of the extraordinary conspiracy which the late Diogenes Patroclos had developed without sharing any of its threads completely with anyone.

"I'm still puzzled about the codebook," she said. "I don't see why he pretended not to know you'd taken it."

Simon lounged back in his chair.

"The codebook was a very interesting, not to say a crucial part of the whole set-up. And of course, it was partly the codebook, in the end, that gave the game away. Remember that what he had in mind when he first briefed me was to get me into contact with his supposed impersonator for just long enough to convince me that there *was* a double. My main job was to get the codebook back. That gave me a specific goal—and it gave him the perfect pretext for hauling me off the job before I got *too* nosey. Once I'd delivered it, he could tell me to quit—"

"Of course," broke in the girl. "And that's why he faked the telegram from Athens—or I suppose he had my namesake send it—and made sure you saw it."

Simon nodded.

"Exactly."

"But why did he commission you, anyway—I mean the second time, in London—and then insist you stayed in the house?"

"That was an absolute master-stroke. It was a plausible enough move anyway, in the interests of 'security' as he put it, but his real reason was simply to make it easy for me to pinch the codebook. And he knew I'd bite."

"So where did he go wrong?"

"Apart from the weak basic premise, and my scepticism, there was something else. His own vanity—and a kind of melodramatic cloak-and-dagger streak. He *did* keep just one copy of the codebook, as I figure it—"

"Yes, as far as I know. He always took it with him when he went away or out of the house for more than a few hours."

"Well," Simon continued, "when I stole it from his safe, he wanted me to think I'd succeeded in getting it to Athens. But he also wanted it there in London—because he was stuck without it. He could have had it sent back, of course, but he preferred to play games by following me at a distance and bringing it back the same night. But I spotted the car behind, and that was when I really started putting the picture together."

"But what about the photos? A lucky accident, you said?"

He nodded.

"That was one piece of circumstantial evidence he *didn't* manufacture himself. There were two photos—press photos, remember? —with the dates stamped on the back. Both the tenth of June. Dio presenting a yachting trophy in the Bahamas—that was late afternoon—and Dio at a party in Lisbon that same night, maybe six or eight hours later. Or at least, I *assumed* it was that same night. And with the time difference, he'd have had to travel almost instantaneously to get there. And it's three thousand miles."

"So how *can* the photos be explained?" she asked.

"By the fact that the Lisbon one was taken *first*. I saw the photos at the *Daily Express* office, and as the agency names were stamped on the backs along with the dates, I was able to phone them and check. As I'd suspected, the Lisbon agency always dates its prints the day they're processed. Normally that's almost at once. But a picture taken during the night—say, at a party—is pretty certain to carry the *next* day's date."

"I think I'm beginning to see. He went to the party in Lisbon on the night of the ninth—"

"Or you might say, the night of the ninth-tenth. So let's suppose the picture was taken at midnight. He might easily have left for the Bahamas at, say, three in the morning, on the tenth. By my reckoning, he could have gotten there in eighteen or twenty hours without much sweat. Let's say he landed at twenty-two hundred hours. But remember the time-zone change. In Nassau it wasn't ten o'clock at night—it was only four in the afternoon. So he was in time to wave to the out-island yachtsmen."

The Saint stood up and looked at his watch.

"And now I think it's time for that lunch I promised you."

"Just one last question," Ariadne said. "What are you getting out of this?"

He looked at her with imps of mischief dancing in his clear blue eyes. "The excitement of the chase—the satisfaction of a day's work well done—"

"I mean, you were supposed to be paid, weren't you?"

"And what makes you think I haven't been?" he asked with as straight a face as he could muster. "I'll let you into a secret. There are occasions, I'm sorry to say, when I steal more than codebooks. Though it was from the codebook that I copied down an interesting-looking series of figures." He turned his most innocent gaze on her and added, "And do you know what those figures turned out to be?"

Ariadne shook her head, and Simon grinned.

"The combination to a safe—the one right behind you, in fact."

He patted his breast pocket meaningly, and the girl's eyes widened.

"You helped yourself?"

"Shamelessly," replied the Saint. "To forty thousand pounds in conveniently large-demonination Swiss franc notes."

"Forty thousand! But . . . you said your fee was to be *twenty* thousand!"

Simon Templar looked aggrieved.

"But I was commissioned for that sum twice," he pointed out. "Twenty thousand from Patroclos One, twenty thousand from Patroclos Two. Wasn't it lucky that they turned out to share a safe?"

And he smiled his incorrigible mocking smile.

"Come on—let's go and get that lunch," said the Saint.

II.

The Pawn Gambit

CHAPTER 1

On a certain grey afternoon in November of that year—traditionally a month when depression and despair sink to their nadir—a short balding man with an exclusive legal right to the name of Albert Nobbins was walking dejectedly by the Serpentine in London's Hyde Park.

There was rain in the air, and no one else was visible in the park except a few dutiful dog-walkers dotted about way over beyond the far side of the lake. Nobbins walked with an aimless and plodding gait, faltering frequently like a man with scarcely more incentive to move forward than to go back, or to stand still. His purposeless steps took him along the lakeside path because that was the way he always went; and he was walking there in the park, not because he had anywhere in particular to go, nor even with the object of exercising his small flabby body, but because it was his habit, and because there was nothing else he could think of to do.

He neither saw nor heard the black car that slowed to a crawl on the road some fifty yards obliquely behind him. But even if he had seen or heard it, he was too deeply sunk in melancholy thought to pay it any special attention, and too far away from it to see the heavy revolver which the man in the back seat was toying with, almost affectionately. . . .

Some men are Winners, gifted with every advantage in the scramble of life that nature and nurture with their most munificent combined efforts can supply. The Winner is that rare man who seems to lead a charmed life right from the beginning. As an infant, he never knows what it is to be short of a lollipop. His schoolboy marbles invariably conquer and multiply, and he attacks a ball with various conventional implements with seemingly innate dexterity. Later, his girl friends are abundantly plural and pulchritudinous; he reaps sporting or academic honours, or both, by the dozen; and plum jobs drop into his lap even when he hasn't exerted himself beyond the effort of sitting under the tree.

Success, recognition, popularity, money, affection, all through his life the Winner seems to attract them with nonchalant ease. He enjoys a distinguished and rewarding career, leading a blamelessly honourable existence and in due season breeding tribes of children and grandchildren—themselves doubtless including a goodly proportion of Winners.

Now to someone whose outlook as a respectable dutiful citizen has been perverted by exposure to some heretical scepticism about the Establishment, this picture of fulfilled felicity will undeniably seem tinged with dullness around at least some of its edges. Albert Nobbins, however, as he plodded along by the Serpentine on that damp grey November day, could contemplate it only with envy.

Nobbins was a Loser—an insignificant little man whose failures seemed to him as congenital as a Winner's successes. As if it were not enough to have inherited such a risible cognomen as Nobbins, his parents had compounded his misfortune by linking it with one of the most unglamorous of Christian names. And from that depressing start, his fortune was apparently foredoomed. Lollipops, marbles, girls, success in sport or studies or career, were all one to Albert Nobbins: they had all evaded him as if by some inexorable magnetic repulsion. And despite his most desperate endeavours, his attempts to wield a bat or club or racquet had been so far removed from any semblance of style that onlookers were invariably reduced to laughter.

He could hear that cruel laughter still, more than forty years on.

He stopped and stared glumly at the water; half a dozen ducks scudded hopefully towards him and converged on a spot a few yards from the bank, the distance which they knew from experience to be the average crust-tossing range of the general public. But Albert Nobbins shook his head at them abstractedly, and they dispersed as he plodded on with the same short, somehow inefficient steps. An insignificant little man, plump and balding and bespectacled, who every morning shaved his face to the same pink well-scrubbed shininess.

He had always been acutely resentful of his puny physique. He knew it was one of the roots of his lack of confidence, and he knew that his lack of confidence in turn explained his lifelong failures. He had no presence. Nobody noticed him; and the ultimate result of that was that whatever potentialities he might have had to be positive, assertive—*effective*—had been stunted. But buried within him was a smouldering core of angry rebellion: buried less deeply now than at any time in his life, but still unsuspected by nearly everyone who knew him. He had ability and diligence— enough to have served his country in positions of modest responsibility and trust (as he might have put it himself), but he was bitterly conscious of how much he might have done but hadn't, of how much of him was unfulfilled.

A few spots of heavier rain splattered down. Nobbins turned up the collar of his fawn gabardine raincoat and walked on. He lived nearby in a small bachelor flat in Knightsbridge, and had made a habit of walking in the park for an hour or so whenever he had an afternoon free. If it rained, he got wet: a trivial matter to a confirmed Loser, a man born—and a sardonic smile flickered briefly on his lips as the phrase occurred to him—born with a cardboard spoon in his mouth. And what was a spot of rain to a man who had just lived out six weeks in the shadow of The Squad? He had been through nobody-knew-what agonies of fear—always conscious that he might be exposed at any moment, never knowing when sentence would be passed on him, when the blow would fall, the final deadly shots ring out. . . . He was like a man too afraid of heights even to ride upstairs in a double-decker bus, but who had walked the circus high wire, and had somehow, miraculously, survived. But it was on a note of failure that he had left The Squad behind him. He had been replaced. And now he felt slack and washed out. Failure again. Always the same story.

He walked on, his thoughts a bitter recapitulation spanning his whole life; and he cursed again the malignity of the fates which had condemned him to imprisonment in that small ineffectual body.

The black car was still moving near-silently at a slow pace, keep-

ing the same relative position behind Nobbins and to the side of
him. The driver, a raw-boned hard-faced Scot, put down the binoculars for which he had momentarily taken his eyes off the road.

"Aye, that's him right enough." He glanced backwards at the
handsome tough-looking man behind him, a man with a shock of
dark hair, longer side-whiskers than the general fashion, and a
bandit's moustache. "All right, Gascott. You know what to do."

Gascott's lips curled back briefly in a cursory smile which somehow combined anticipatory relish with cold contempt, and he
nodded once.

"Yes, Lembick. I know what to do. Bang bang bang."

And Gascott laughed, a cold metallic laugh.

"Get on with it then!" Lembick snapped. He fiercely resented
Gascott's superior assurance; and so did Cawber, the square and
equally taciturn passenger beside him who was now nursing a cum-
bersome cine camera.

Cawber spoke.

"Okay, let's see if you're as cool out there as you're smart in
here."

The voice proclaimed Cawber's New York origins, and the sentence was among the longest Gascott had heard him utter.

Gascott seemed totally at his ease, his relaxation as tangible as
Lembick and Cawber's tension. He took a long silencer out of his
pocket and fitted it to the revolver with calm efficiency, almost
caressing it into position. The job took just a few moments, yet
his actions seemed completely unhurried.

He let the gun swing round carelessly, till it pointed almost
straight at the American's ear.

"Nice long string of words, Cawber—for you!" he sneered. Gascott's harsh yet cultured voice suggested both his ruthlessness and
an army-officer background. "You're getting almost fluent."

Cawber caught the gun by its silencer and twisted it savagely
aside.

"Just remember, Gascott," he growled. "We'll be watching.
And tonight"—he tapped the cine camera with a stubby forefinger
—"so will Rockham. So you just better be sure and get it right."

Gascott leaned over and flicked a lever on the cine camera.

"You'd better get your own end of it right. We wouldn't want

the film running backwards, would we? And don't forget the telephoto lens."

Gascott tucked the gun into a deep inside pocket of his dark
raincoat; and even before Lembick had brought the car completely to a halt, he had opened the door and was gone.

Gascott was a man who had passed through many schools of violence, a man to whom sudden death was a far from unfamiliar
experience, who had faced as well as delivered it down the barrels
of many assorted guns. But only a few weeks before, he had
known nothing of Lembick, or Cawber, or Rockham, and he
might well have found it hard to believe that on this grey November afternoon he would be carrying out The Squad's death sentence on Albert Nobbins.

Lembick and Cawber watched with viciously grudging approval
as his tall figure crossed the grass with easy strides, in a course that
made a shallow angle with the path along which Nobbins's much
shorter steps were taking him. It was Lembick and Cawber's fierce
hope that Gascott would fudge the job; but they had seen enough
of him in training to be virtually certain they would be disappointed; and they festered with an impotent smouldering rancour
at the thought of his growing prestige with Rockham.

"Smart ass!"

Cawber spat out the words as he screwed a telephoto lens to the
camera turret and wound down the car window. He rested the
heavy camera on the window-ledge and squinted through the
viewfinder, keeping Gascott's long-striding form in the small
centre square which represented the magnified field of view.

Gascott reached the path about twenty yards behind Nobbins,
and rapidly began to close the gap. Lembick stopped the car and
raised the binoculars to his eyes; Cawber started the camera.

Neither man heard the well-muffled shots, but Lembick saw the
elongated revolver twitch three times in Gascott's steady hand.
With the first shot, Nobbins seemed to stop, as if there was something he had suddenly remembered; and then, as the other two
shots went home, he crumpled, pitched forward on his face, and
lay still.

Lembick continued to watch for a few moments as a dark stain
slowly spread through Nobbins's coat, just above the centre of his

back. Then, with a further glance around to establish that none of the distant figures in the park who were nobly getting wet in the cause of canine indulgence had noticed anything untoward, he drove the car forward till it was level with Gascott.

And Gascott came back across the grass with the same long measured strides, no whit more hurried than before.

As soon as the tall gunman had eased himself back into the car, Lembick drove smartly away. Gascott unscrewed the silencer and put it back in his pocket.

"Any criticisms—gentlemen?" he said, giving the final word a satirical intonation that made it an insult.

"Nothing much wrong with that," Lembick said shortly. The words seemed wrong from his lips. "A professional job, I'd say." After a pause he added: "Are you quite sure he's dead, though?"

"With three bullets through the heart, would you be planning your next year's holiday—laddie?"

Lembick nodded, keeping himself under control with visible difficulty.

"All right, we know you're a good shot," he said harshly. "We've seen you on the range."

Gascott turned to Cawber.

"What about Alfred Hitchcock's opinion?" he rasped.

Cawber glowered.

"I guess you did a pretty good job. But you—you shoulda gotten closer."

"But that would have been too easy. You know—unsporting!"

Gascott laughed, and Cawber and Lembick eyed him malevolently. He knew exactly the line of English gentlemanly phraseology calculated to incense them both.

"No, no," he went on, "that certainly wouldn't have been playing the game. No real target practice at all! But don't you worry about Mike Argyle—he's not going to be in our hair any more."

There was a terrible calm finality in Gascott's last sentence that chilled even the hardened trainers of The Squad.

"Well, anyway Rockham should be pleased enough," Lembick grunted, still controlling his antagonism with an effort.

Again Gascott's chilling laugh rang out.

"Poor old Mike—a posthumous film star!" But if you're good

boys," he rasped, "I'll ask Rockham to let you bring around the ice creams in the interval."

It was Albert Nobbins they had left lying there face down in the mud, with the rain pattering onto his back. But the men of The Squad knew him only as Mike Argyle, a name he had chosen for himself as more befitting the sort of personage he would have liked to be, under which he had lived among them for the six fear-ridden weeks of his masquerade.

Likewise, the man who had fired the gun was known to The Squad as George Gascott, and by no other name. But to some, despite the changes in his appearance, voice, and manner, he would have been recognisable as Simon Templar—more widely known as "the Saint."

CHAPTER 2

The three weeks Simon Templar had spent in Brixton Prison were among the longest in his memory.

For more years than he cared to count, the police of at least half a dozen countries around the world had been longing to put the Saint behind bars; while for his part the Saint—whose preference was decidedly for the kind of bars that dispense liquid conviviality—had just as consistently declined to gratify their policemanly yearnings.

Despite their best endeavours, he had never yet heard a prison gate clang shut behind him.

Until the events that were begun by Pelton's phone call.

"Simon Templar?" said the clipped precise voice. "Pelton. David Pelton. Colonel. I expect you'll remember me." And as Simon groped through his memory the voice went on with the same brisk precision. "We met, as I recall, three times. The last occasion was just under six years ago. You were serving with some cloak-and-dagger outfit under a bloke named Hamilton, and I was one of your London contacts. You'll remember that I was then— as indeed I still am now—in one of the"—here the voice paused fractionally—"Government departments."

Simon remembered. The mention of Hamilton struck a chord of memory which he hoped would never be altogether silent. He remembered those days in a war-torn world when he had enjoyed a commission as tenuously legal as anything in his highly illegal career; days when, in the midst of war, he had known a paradoxical peace, a unique pride in his own functioning and that of friend and comrade. He seldom thought back to those days—they belonged to another life—but he could never forget them. And

Pelton's words made them come back to him now with a sudden vivid clarity.

"Yes, of course I remember," he said easily. "One of the . . . lesser-known departments, isn't it?"

"Quite so." Pelton went straight on as if he had planned out exactly what he was going to say, down to the last unspoken comma. "Look here, Simon—I may call you Simon?—I'll come straight to the point, as far as that's possible in advance. I'm authorised to make you a proposition, which I hope you'll consider seriously. Can you come to my office in the morning?"

Pelton quite properly refused to give any particulars over the phone, except to say that what he wanted to talk about was a temporary job which the Saint might well find irresistible. Simon declared bluntly that as a free spirit whose days of legal employment had ended with the war, by his own decision, he was likely to find it all too resistible. But Pelton pointed out that he could lose nothing by hearing the details, and Simon had to agree. In truth he had made up his mind at once to hear them. His curiosity would never have let him do otherwise.

But curiosity was as far as it would go, he told himself with conviction as, next morning, he weaved the big Hirondel in and out of the London traffic on his way to the appointment. Simon Templar was first and last his own man, and just then he could think of no peacetime circumstances that might persuade him to surrender a slice of his independence for the dubious pleasure of working for Pelton's intelligence department.

The address Pelton had given him was one of those dull characterless office buildings off Whitehall in which some of the more shabbily anonymous Government enterprises are housed, or concealed. Simon was struck by how little the man he remembered had altered in the intervening years. The hair was maybe a half-shade greyer, the lines etched into his alert face perhaps fractionally deeper; but he was the same odd birdlike man, with a scrawny neck, a scrubby moustache, and a habit of cocking his head on one side as he spoke. Simon had had little to do with him personally in those days—there had been just the three brief meetings Pelton had mentioned on the phone—but he knew that the colonel's rather stiff military manner hid an astute brain and an often startling unorthodoxy of approach. Or so his reputation had insisted.

Once the inevitable tea ceremony was over, Pelton dismissed his secretary with a curt nod and a flick of the hand. Then he leaned back in his chair, put his neatly manicured fingertips together, and studied the Saint with his small dark eyes. They had a peculiar glittering brightness which completed the birdlike effect.

"According to the rule-book," he began half-apologetically, "I ought to remind you—though I don't imagine it's really necessary in your case—that you signed the Official Secrets Act nine years ago—"

"And when you sign, you sign for life," supplied the Saint succinctly.

"Quite so." Pelton paused, with his head cocked sideways in his characteristic manner. "I'll come straight to the point, then. "Does the name John Rockham mean anything to you?"

Simon shook his head.

"Never heard of him. Sounds like a boxer, or someone who should have a diamond named after him. What's his line of business?"

"His line of business, as you put it," Pelton said in his rather precise tones, "involves masterminding a nasty little—or not so little—organisation of ex-military and criminal misfits. Even if you've never heard of Rockham himself, I think you may well have heard of The Squad."

"The Squad . . . ?" A furrow appeared fleetingly in the Saint's brow as he tried to recall something that had been printed only lightly on his memory. "Wait a minute—it does ring a bell. Those three big bank raids in the summer. Rumour had it, in the unorthodox circles in which I sometimes move, that a gang calling themselves The Squad were responsible. And the same gang were credited with that lulu of a currency snatch at the airport."

"Your information came from . . . underworld sources?" inquired Pelton, and the Saint nodded.

"Heard it on the grapevine. But I've been abroad—so I've had fewer lines open than usual. Or should it be tendrils?"

Pelton regarded Simon soberly.

"What else did the grapevine have to say about The Squad?"

"Just that it's some sort of highly drilled private army. Everything run like a military operation—and they specialise in uniformed strikes. The bank jobs were all on the same pattern—four men dressed in the bank security company's uniforms and driving their vans, if you please. It was neat, slick, and thoroughly professional," said the Saint, who gave credit where it was due. "And they got away with oodles of boodle."

Pelton sighed heavily, and inclined his head at an even more avian angle.

"If only Rockham's enterprise stopped there," he said ruefully. "We'd be more than happy to let the usual authorities deal with him and his cohorts. In fact we—I mean SIS—would never have needed to become involved at all. But Rockham's more than just a very enterprising criminal leader. There have been—other jobs."

"What sort of jobs?"

"Jobs your grapevine won't have attributed to The Squad. For the simple reason that they never got into the papers."

"I'm interested," said the Saint flatly. "Give me a for instance."

A ripple of discomfort ruffled the surface of Pelton's businesslike self-possession.

"For a start," he said, "army stores. Five raids in all, in various parts of the country. One was an ordnance depot. They've all been hushed up, with considerable difficulty."

It took the Saint several incredulous moments to find his voice.

"You're not seriously telling me they've raided *the army?*"

"I'm not in the habit of making jokes of that sort," Pelton replied drily.

"Naturally not," Simon said with a completely straight face. "What did they get away with?"

Pelton counted the items off on the fingers of one hand.

"An assortment of uniforms—various regiments. Enough of the latest weaponry to equip The Squad twice over—and we reckon there are about fifty of them all told. Plenty of ammunition to go with the firearms. Three three-ton lorries. And two jeeps."

The Saint expressed himself in a long soundless whistle.

"There was also the little matter of a high-speed naval launch taken at gunpoint from Portsmouth Harbour," Pelton went on. "Apart from which there have been two raids on police stations in the home counties. The Squad emerged with a couple of brand-new police Wolseleys and a dozen and a half assorted uniforms. All ranks below Assistant Commissioner."

"How embarrassing for our boys in blue," murmured the Saint. "Ye gods, but the man has nerve!" There was a note of something almost like respect in Simon Templar's voice. "The very citadels of Law and Order in its most capital-letter solemnity! Even I, in my most youthful exuberance, never went so far as to actually hold up a citadel of Law and Order. They did hold them up, I suppose?"

Pelton nodded, shrugging as he did so.

"And do you mean to say," continued the Saint, "that all these raided parties surrendered their uniforms and whatnot without a murmur? I'd love to have seen those bobbies, waving goodbye in their underwear—"

"It's true that most of the people concerned as victims of these raids were completely taken by surprise," Pelton said with total earnestness. "It isn't every day, for example, that the police manning a fairly small station are suddenly faced with a dozen or more men armed with tommy-guns. There was very little they could have done, in the circumstances. There was, as you say, no fight. Except at the ordnance depot."

"And what happened there?"

"Rockham lost two men—out of perhaps twenty-five. The army lost twelve," Pelton said quietly; and the Saint grew suddenly very sober.

"I'm sorry if I seemed flippant just now," he said with a grim quietness that matched Pelton's own.

For a long moment the fighting lines of Simon Templar's jaw tightened and there was a frozen sapphire glint in his eyes that went a long way to explain his well-attested capacity for arousing an unholy fear among even the most hard-bitten specimens of humanity.

"The Squad's tough outfit, all right," Pelton said. "But even that isn't the half of it, Simon. Rockham's nobody's fool, and as far as we can tell, all these jobs—as well as some less spectacular ones—in fact virtually everything he's done in the year or so since he started—has been of a preparatory nature. Recruiting, training, equipping—consolidation of military resources, you might call it."

Simon wouldn't have called it any such thing; but he conquered the urge to say so, and instead asked the obvious question.

"What are The Squad preparing *for?*"

"Contract work," said Pelton. "You see, Rockham regards himself as the leader, not just of a criminal gang, but of a troop of mercenary commandos. A trained group of ruthless fighting men for hire. And he's not fussy about who'd hire them."

Simon Templer had been in the business long enough to know that the fount of criminal enterprise would never dry up. There always would be brand-new rackets, and new variants of old ones, for as long as there were villains left in the world to dream them up; and for this fact of life he had been known to offer fervent thanks to whatever gods might be appointed to watch over the interests of free-lance buccaneers. Without the mercifully inexhaustible springs of villainy, life for Simon Templar might have soon got boring. True, the present vista was little more than a promising monochrome preview, but there was a part of the Saint's consciousness that responded directly to the emanations of adventure, like a finely tuned radio receiver. It was a pity, Simon mused, that he'd made up his mind in advance to turn down whatever assignment it was that Pelton was planning to offer. . . .

He pondered awhile, trying to put together some background out of what he knew about the mercenary game.

"What's your definition of a mercenary?" he asked, and Pelton inclined his head and replied with his usual precision.

"In the normal sense, a mercenary soldier is one who fights under a foreign flag for payment, in the form of wages or of spoils, or both."

Simon nodded thoughtfully.

"That's more or less what I'd have said. Though I've a kind of feeling it leaves something out."

"It certainly does in the case of The Squad. Although we've reason to believe that some of Rockham's men have fought abroad, the *modus operandi* he seems to prefer is rather different. He prefers to take his orders, or commissions, not from a foreign military commander, but from the foreign power's intelligence agents—in this country."

Simon Templar sat up slowly in his chair.

"You mean from—what I believe you people call the other side?"

"Hostile or potentially hostile powers, yes." Pelton was bland and matter-of-fact. "As I said, The Squad are not fussy."

"And these commissions—what sort of commissions?"

Pelton spread his well-tended hands.

"Whatever dirty work they want done. Theft of U. K. Government property and information. Political abduction. Jailbreaks. Assassination—you'll remember the shooting of the American Trade Attaché last month . . ."

"That was The Squad again?"

"We're ninety-nine percent certain."

"Where's The Squad based?" he asked.

"On a big country estate in the wilds of Hampshire, not far from Petersfield. It used to be a public school, and before that a stately home. Ideal for Rockham's purposes. Ostensibly he runs it as a kind of exclusive health farm, to discourage too many local questions."

"And the place is well guarded, I suppose?"

"A veritable fortress. High walls, barbed-wire fences, armed patrols, dogs—the lot."

"Why not drop a bomb on it?" suggested the Saint pragmatically.

Pelton ran a hand through his sparse grey hair and sighed with the resigned patience of a civil servant accustomed to the bureaucratic brakes that inhibit his enterprise.

"There are times," he said, "when I really do envy you freelancers your scope for direct action. Of course we could smash The Squad out of existence in a matter of minutes, if we chose. And you can imagine how the army are chafing at the bit, after their own contact with The Squad. But the fact is, we daren't break up the organisation just yet—not until we know a good bit more about it. So far we're by no means certain The Squad *is* the entire organisation—or even its centre."

"No point in cutting off a tentacle and leaving the octopus," ventured the Saint.

"Exactly. There's still a great deal we don't know. As I said,

Rockham's information is good. Our own is less good. Which is where you come in—if you'll do it. We badly need a man on the inside, Simon."

"An infiltrator?" The Saint's lazy blue eyes searched Pelton's face. "But why me? There must be plenty of first-class agents in SIS, and several in your own department who'd be suitable. What about Randall, for instance? This assignment might have been tailor-made for him."

Simon's reference was to Jack Randall, one of his most affectionately remembered wartime colleagues, an American anglophile who had joined Pelton's department after the peace.

"In my opinion, you're the best man for the job," Pelton said candidly, but also with a hint of evasion which, at the time, Simon only half-registered. "Though in view of your reputation I had the devil of a time convincing the red-tape wallahs at the Ministry, I can tell you. And even more of a job persuading them to sanction a fee that wouldn't strike you as totally derisory."

"Don't tell me the amount," said the Saint quickly. "It won't make any difference. I'm afraid I'm not taking the job. I won't deny I'm fascinated—and tempted—by the thought of coming to grips with this cross between Al Capone and the Foreign Legion, and I won't deny that I'm flattered. But I'm a free-lancer through and through. So thanks—but I did warn you," he ended rather lamely.

Somehow, having said all that, the Saint was uneasily aware that something still remained to be said, or asked. Maybe it had to do with the fact that Pelton looked less disappointed than he ought to have done—as if, for him, the game was not yet lost.

And that was when Simon remembered the faint note of evasion that had crept into Pelton's voice. Somewhere there had been something out of place, or out of time, or micrometrically out of focus. . . .

And then suddenly, before he had groped even halfway to an answer, he was chilled by an icy wind of apprehension; and he found himself almost by instinct steering the conversation towards its source.

"I'm afraid you'll just have to use one of your own men after all," he told Pelton in a voice that outran his conscious mind.

"But I daren't," Pelton said. "At least, not a frontline man. For all we know, Rockham may even have photos of some of our regular operators—of one of the Opposition's intelligence. I can't take that risk. Whereas you—your face would never be associated with us now. And besides, the cover I have in mind for you involves an element of disguise—"

"Well, if your infiltrator's appearance is going to be altered anyway, I can't see that there'd be any special risk of recognition," Simon put in reasonably. "And as it happens, Randall's an expert in that line, as he proved in France. Why not let him have a crack at it? Or is he busy elsewhere?"

Pelton hesitated for a long moment; and when he spoke Simon knew that the evasion had been real.

"No, he's not busy," Pelton said with deliberate calm. "Prepare yourself for a shock, Simon. I'm afraid Randall has already met The Squad."

The Saint went very still.

"What's happened to him?" he asked levelly; but he had a premonition of what the answer would be.

"Randall is dead. You'll remember there always was a streak of recklessness in him. He insisted on going over the wall, down at Rockham's HQ, to see what he could nose out. His body was fished out of the Thames a week ago. Unidentifiable—except by a secret mark known to us."

CHAPTER 3

It was as if a flash-bulb had been exploded in front of Simon Templar's eyes. For a while he scarcely saw the man before him, and yet certain details registered mechanically on the film of his memory, so that as much as a year later he might have been able to picture accurately the exact shape of a patch of chipped-off paint on the skirting board beyond Pelton's desk in that supremely unmemorable office.

He had worked with Randall. And then their paths had diverged, as men's paths do. But to Simon Templar, Randall was a part of the memory of those days when he had found another kind of satisfaction, as complete in its way as any he had known before or since, when Simon and Randall and others had forged links of mutual respect and brotherhood amid the often hair-raising exigencies of their exploits with the French resistance workers. Frenchman and American and Briton had spoken for once in the same accents, the accents of determination and freedom. Men had been bonded then in a kind of loyalty that only the menace of a common enemy can cement; and it was understood as an inevitable fact of life, and not to be questioned, that when one brave man fell, any of his friends and comrades would step forward to take his place, with a purpose made only more firm by the knowledge of the risks involved . . .

And now Randall was dead.

It never even occurred to the Saint that he still had a choice. Almost mechanically, he repeated that the amount of the proffered fee was irrelevant, but said that he would take the job.

Only afterwards was it fully borne in upon him how skilfully Pelton had played the news of Randall's death, like a high trump kept till the last card. He must have known enough about the

kind of man Simon Templar was, and about his likely reactions,
to be fairly doubtful of enlisting his aid, so he had saved his biggest gun for the moment when its effect would be most immediately and hopefully decisive.

This said something for Pelton's strategic talents—which duly
went up a couple of notches in the Saint's estimation—but it also
bespoke a degree of cold-blooded calculation which cast doubt on
his more sympathetic façade, which duly went down the same scale
by a similar amount.

But that was after Simon had had a chance, later, to sit down
and think about it soberly. At the time, he was carried along in
the bitter wake of that final news of Randall. The Saint was spoil-
ing for a fight, and he was in no mood to wait.

But he was about as far from overjoyed as it is possible to be
when Pelton told him that his cover as George Gascott would
take an absolute minimum of four weeks to establish, and that he
would have to spend three of them in jail.

Patience had never been one of Simon Templar's outstanding
virtues. He was inclined to be impatient in particular with the
way things are done in official, as opposed to privateering, circles.
It often seemed to him that the processes whereby officialdom
ground out its slow results were mostly characterised by a degree
of lead-footedness beside which a palsied geriatric snail battling
through thick treacle against a strong headwind would have
seemed to be positively zipping along.

Which is merely one way of pointing out that if The Squad
had been purely the Saint's own party, and Rockham's base a private target for his own brand of freebooting vengeance, he would
probably have figured out another way of setting about it.

However, given the central principle of an infiltrator, he had to
admit that Pelton's cover idea was a good one. And he had to
agree, too, that a month was the least possible time it could take
him to perfect himself in the role he had to play.

Nobody applied to join The Squad: Rockham selected. And the
evidence was that anyone who got as far as a final interview and
was then rejected, or turned the job down, found it extraordinarily
difficult to talk about it, on account of being dead.

Presumably Rockham made good use of certain official documents which were easily enough available to anyone who knew of their existence and only took the trouble to get hold of them. For a start, he would certainly study the periodic lists of newly released convicts and of dishonourable service discharges.

And presumably too, he had access like the Saint to some of the shifting subterranean networks which carry information of a less official and more guarded kind. Doubtless he would usually come to hear of it before long when a potentially suitable man was, criminally speaking, at a loose end. . . .

Anyhow, whatever his sources, Rockham managed to find a hunting ground of potential recruits. Within it he then applied his own rigorous standards of selection. Physical fitness and courage were not enough; he only took men who gave evidence of having already developed the prime mercenary qualities—tough ruthlessness and unscrupulous venality—to an advanced level.

George Gascott matched up to the prescription very well. To be irresistible to Rockham, all the Saint had to do was step into Gascott's identity.

Now in his late thirties, as a younger man George Gascott had held the King's Commission in the Commandos for several years; until His Majesty decided, or someone decided on His Majesty's behalf, that in spite of Captain Gascott's undeniable military efficiency, the commission could be terminated with advantage to His Majesty, the Royal Marines, and the tax-paying public. Some of the latter's money—by an ingenious and complicated inventory fraud involving nonexistent equipment—had almost certainly found its way into the suave Gascott's pockets. Though the fraud was technically unprovable, fortunately for His Majesty *et al* a fight in which Gascott half-killed a fellow officer supplied a good enough reason for a parting of the ways.

After that, Gascott had spent a few years in the Far East, and the records made it clear that nobody knew what he had done during the war or when exactly he had re-entered Britain. But Simon remembered how a big Hatton Garden robbery had hit the news three years ago, and how the grapevine in those days had named Gascott as masterminding it.

And if Gascott hadn't had the sheer bad luck to be picked on for a random customs search at Dover, he would have got clean away with the £50,000 worth of diamonds they found on him. That was a quarter of the Hatton Garden haul, and he steadfastly refused to say what had happened to the rest.

He was sent down for ten years: the robbery, as the judge remarked, had been one of the most brutal and bloody as well as one of the most lucrative of recent years. But they never got Gascott as far as the prison gates. Somehow, almost miraculously, he escaped from the Black Maria in which they were taking him there; and this time he did get out of the country. No one knew how much of the remaining boodle he took with him.

Rockham would certainly approve of comrade Gascott, the Saint felt sure of that. Except maybe for the one flaw which rather marred the glory of his escape.

He had been recaptured.

That few of Scotland Yard's representatives are overgifted with imagination is a fact which this dutiful chronicler has sometimes been obliged to record, however painful it may have been to himself. However, what they may lack in vision they amply make up for in doggedness; and recently their low-key but persistent search for Gascott had paid off. They had found him in Rio de Janeiro; he had been extradited; and now he was somewhere on the Atlantic Ocean, on his way back. He was sharing a cabin with three of the said dogged representatives, and it is a matter of record that they were watching him very closely indeed.

His arrival at Tilbury, a week after Pelton's meeting with the Saint, brought a predictable splash of front-page newspaper coverage, including photographs of the man who was on his way to Brixton to serve the sentence he should have begun three years before. But for some reason the mug-shots which the authorities saw fit to release were of a photographic quality rivalling the results of Aunt Mabel's efforts with a box camera on a misty evening.

Pelton had quietly gone aboard with the pilot; and when Gascott disembarked three hours later any direct contact with the aggrieved gentlemen of the press was precluded by his posture and his condition, which were respectively horizontal and delirious.

The fuzzy photographs were of Simon Templar, complete with new hairstyle and hastily grown moustache; and the fuzziness was a necessary precaution against the potential puzzled squawking of any of Gascott's friends, relatives, or victims who might have detected the substitution—or for that matter of any zealous newspaperman or policeman who wasn't privy to Pelton's plan.

The reports accompanying the fuzzy photos gave lurid details of his exploits and ascribed his horizontality and delirium to a violent bout of malaria, a recurring legacy of his time in Malaya. Accordingly, the reports continued, he would not be going straight to Brixton but would be "kept under observation" for a few days in another prison hospital.

Actually he was taken to one of Pelton's "safe houses," and Simon Templar was taken there too.

"There's more than a remote chance," Pelton pointed out, "that once you get into The Squad—assuming you do—you'll meet someone who's known Gascott, at some time. If your cover's going to stand up to that kind of test, you'll need to be equipped to give a pretty convincing impersonation."

And the Saint knew that Pelton was right. It didn't have to be perfect—anyone Simon was likely to run into who had known Gascott before would probably not have seen him for several years —but it had to be pretty good.

That was why he met the real George Gascott and spent three days almost constantly in his company. They talked about anything that might help him to get an insight into Gascott's character; which meant that they talked about almost anything under the sun, but in particular about his military experience and his shadier contacts. And all the time, throughout those three days, Simon was also studying, consciously and osmotically, Gascott's distinctive voice and smoothly arrogant manner.

He couldn't find much to like in Gascott. There was just one saving grace as far as the Saint was concerned: Gascott was not without humour; and at times, when just for a while the sadistic edge was missing, it was a humour something like the Saint's own. For which he was grateful, because it would make the part just that bit less onerous to keep up.

In the three days he got everything he usefully could have got out of personal contact; and then there was no need to extend that contact any longer. He took his leave of Gascott with considerable relief, and went away with a sheaf of notes which promised to keep him well occupied in his prison cell.

When he entered that cell for the first time, on the following day, the real George Gascott remained in relatively comfortable lodgings at the safe house, well guarded but consoled by the promise that in return for his cooperation, when he was eventually transferred to an ordinary prison, his very first application for parole would be granted.

It had been no sweat for Pelton, talking Gascott into it. Once he had got over an understandable initial suspicion, Gascott had agreed at once. It meant that his aborted escape would not be held against him, and complete freedom would be brought very close; and in return all he had to do was agree to the loan of his identity for an undisclosed purpose. That was the bargain. And Gascott was more than content with it.

Simon Templar, on the other hand, was soon feeling every bit as restless and discontented as he had known he would. Prison life did not agree with him. He hated the routine, he hated the meals, and most of all he hated being cooped up.

True, he was rather a special prisoner. The needs of his mission dictated a semi-solitary confinement. Though he ate with the others, he took his exercise sessions alone in the concrete prison quadrangle—or alone except for the four armed warders—and was otherwise kept very much to his small single cell. Gascott's record, fortunately, made these arrangements seem plausible enough to avoid raising suspicion among any of the fellow inmates.

The move of the supposed "Gascott" to Brixton from the unnamed hospital where he had recovered from his bout of malaria had not gone unreported; and even though at that period no system of morning deliveries of the newspapers to those detained at His Majesty's pleasure had yet been implemented, still the word sped around and there was scarcely a man in the prison on the day after his arrival who didn't know that the tall newcomer with something of the look of a pirate or gypsy about him was George Gascott.

Only he wasn't.

Simon Templar had to admit that the physical discomfort he was enduring in Gascott's stead was less than extreme. The food was an affront to his educated palate, but doubtless it supplied an adequate minimum of sustenance and was a whole lot better than bread-and-water rations would have been. And the cell was hardly reminiscent of the Bastille; it was a light-painted room, simple and functional, with a narrow bed, a table, and a chair—all solidly made and bolted firmly to the floor. And there was a washbasin, with cold water. The conditions were plain and spartan rather than punitive in themselves.

But the loss of liberty: that was real enough to the Saint, and there were times when he paced back and forth in his cell like a caged panther, and times when he found himself gazing up through the high barred window for long minutes at the rectangular patch of sky beyond, now blue, now grey, now star-scattered. And then he thought of the men in prisons the world over, the generations of the incarcerated, many of them with little or no prospect of ever being released, for whom that tantalising rectangle of barred sky must have stood as the ever-present symbol of both despair and hope through seemingly interminable years. Educationally, it was quite an experience.

And as he remembered how well off he was in comparison, to be committed to spending only about three weeks there before the escape which he would be allowed to make, he said severe words to himself and went on with preparatory work which would occupy him for that period.

In his seclusion it was easy for him to be given discreet privileges in the form of books and, as Pelton had promised, anything else within reason and practicality that he needed towards those preparations. One of the things he asked for was a chess set; and with this and some esoteric tomes on the subject, he spent hour after hour in engrossed intellectual contemplation. It was years since he had played the game, but chess was one of Gascott's passions—and reputedly one of Rockham's.

In his first week he had two visitors.

One was the "girl friend" Pelton had organised after discovering that there were no genuine friends or relatives of Gascott's on the scene who were on good enough terms to want to see him. In that all-male stronghold the idea of a visiting "girl friend," even one of Pelton's choosing, was something Simon was happy enough to go along with, and he was glad he had done so when he saw her.

Her name was Ruth Barnaby, and she was a member of Pelton's department. She had dark-brown chestnutty hair immaculately coiffured in an upswept style, and the kind of good looks no woman can get out of a bottle or tube or jar, because they depend on the right bone structure. Either you have it or you haven't; and Ruth Barnaby decidedly had it.

She had been well primed. She greeted him through the wire-mesh grille, for the benefit of the warders and fellow inmates present, with exactly the blend of familiarity and restraint that might have been expected of her part; and then she gradually dropped her voice to a level at which it became submerged in the general babble of conversation going on between each of the other men and his visitor and rapidly introduced herself.

"If you manage to get into this group," she told him, "I'll be your local contact down at Kyleham. That's where they're based. We'll need to set up a communication system. You'll be confined to camp for a while, till Rockham thinks you're trustworthy enough to be let off the leash. I suppose you know about all that?"

Simon nodded, aware of the cool grey depths of her eyes.

"David did mention it," he said, keeping his voice well down and maintaining the rasping Gascott tones.

Even though nobody could possibly have picked out what they were saying, it was conceivable that a sharp pair of ears would have registered a complete change in his voice quality and intonation.

The girl gave him a few details about the estate at Kyleham and then left, promising to come back the following week.

The second visitor arrived a couple of days later. Simon had never seen him before. He was a big well-groomed man with a strong square face.

"Mr. Gascott?" he said in a quiet cultured voice. "We haven't met, but I've been reading about you in the newspapers. My name is Rockham—John Rockham."

CHAPTER 4

The Saint was completely and utterly taken aback. He simply hadn't considered the possibility that Rockham might grab at the bait quite as early as that. Yet for all the reaction he showed, the name might have meant absolutely nothing to him.

Which, of course, was no less than Rockham would have expected it to mean to George Gascott.

That the Saint was able to slip naturally and without perceptible delay into the sort of response the real Gascott would have made was entirely to the credit of his acting abilities and to the hard work he had added to them.

"Who the hell are you?" he heard himself rasp at restrained volume just as he had done with the girl. "I told them very distinctly that I could do without any blasted do-gooder namby-pamby professional visitors poking their sanctimonious snouts in."

It gave him an eerie feeling to realise that already, at least as far as outward appearances went, he had all but shrugged himself into Gascott's skin. But that feeling came as a mere fleeting background to the whirling of his brain. Neither he nor Pelton had given any close attention to the problem of how, after his escape, he was going to arrange to be "available" to Rockham. If necessary, in the end, he would simply have presented himself at The Squad's base and played it by ear from them on. Rockham's taking the initiative at this stage—before "Gascott" was actually in a position to be of any use to him—was something that needed thought, and for the moment his mind was racing like a motor out of gear as he tried to fit the new development into some kind of schema he could deal with.

One discomfiting result for the Saint was that he had been caught with half his boning up on the real Gascott's military career still to be done. It was like being stopped in the middle of swotting for tomorrow's exam and summoned to sit it at once; except that this particular test was a practical one that could all too easily, for him, come to resemble nothing so much as picking his way through a minefield. . . .

Rockham said: "I'm no professional visitor"—for a moment the idea seemed to amuse him—"but I am a professional, and in a similar field to your own. I like what I've read about you. I think we've some interests in common."

"I prefer women," sneered the Saint.

Rockham nodded.

"I've done some homework on you," he said ambiguously. "But what I meant was that I want to offer you a job."

Rockham had urbanely ignored the sneer, but the Saint's watchfulness hadn't missed the sparks of anger in Rockham's pale blue eyes; and he knew then that there lay a temper to be reckoned with just beneath that calm and cultivated surface.

And the Saint laughed the cold metallic laugh he had copied with such uncanny accuracy.

"You've come to offer me a job, have you? Well, that's *wonderful* news! I suppose you've brought the rocks with you that you want broken up? Or is it some private mailbags you'd like me to sew?"

Abruptly he dropped the bantering tone and spat out his next words with a bitter savagery:

"I'm in prison, man, prison! Detained at His Majesty's. And when it comes to considering offers of employment, Mister Rockham, I'm just a *trifle* handicapped."

Rockham waited imperturbably for the outburst to subside.

"You'd be worth to me," he said calmly, "two thousand a month. I pay well if I want a man enough. And regarding your present inconvenient predicament"—he paused and flicked his gaze significantly around the visiting-room—"these matters can always be arranged, as you know. I might well be prepared to take a risk to get a man of your calibre on the strength."

The implication was obvious; and it now seemed hardly credible to Simon Templar that he hadn't seen at once, right from the beginning, that there was only the one single postulate on which

Rockham's visit could have made any kind of sense. He was offering to spring Gascott from jail.

In the circumstances the Saint found no difficulty at all in achieving a modest levitation of his eyebrows to express a convincingly surprised-looking realisation.

"You've got the muscle for that, have you?" he said, and the question was halfway to being a statement, a thought spoken aloud by a man busily turning over a proposition in his mind.

"I've got a hundred and three men," said Rockham.

"That's a big outfit."

"And still growing." Rockham's hitherto impassive square features became faintly animated with something Simon assumed to be pride. "We call ourselves The Squad, and we operate on military lines," he explained. "But we're short of leaders—officer material, like yourself. That's why I'm prepared to help you out of your difficulty. Besides which, the exercise'll do the lads good."

Simon appeared to reflect for a moment longer, and then he shook his head decisively.

"The answer's no. I don't want to take a job with anyone who's got a debt to collect from me. It'd cramp my style in the wage negotiations. But how do you know I haven't already made my own arrangements?"

Rockham's cold blue eyes regarded him.

"You've friends on the outside?"

"That's my business. I might have, or I might not. But either way, I've no intention of rotting in this hole for long."

Rockham nodded thoughtfully.

"You did it before," he mused. "Why not again?"

"I'm a clever boy," agreed the Saint.

"I don't doubt it. But you're also a big spender, from what I hear. I'd bet there isn't much left of the Hatton Garden haul, after your three years living it up in Rio. So . . . if and when you fly this coop, Gascott, you may be interested in earning some good money—with prospects of a lot more—for doing the kind of work you'd enjoy."

Rockham stood up.

"You'll find me at Petersfield nine-two-seven-four. But we're in the phone book. The Physical Efficiency Centre, at Kyleham."

Simon Templar breathed a deep sigh of relief when his visitor had gone.

He had been given what amounted to an entrance ticket to The Squad. All he had to do now was to get back to the job of giving himself a chance of surviving once he got there.

In his week-long interlude while the moustachioed Gascott was enjoying Pelton's irregular hospitality, the Saint had not channeled his energies exclusively into nurturing the dark bushy appurtenance that now flourished imitatively on his own upper lip. He had spent much of that week at a certain discreet training centre which is conspicuously absent from the publicly available lists of such Government establishments, working harder than he could remember having worked in a very long time.

Into that week, by some wizardry of frantic compression he marvelled at ever after, was packed course after crash course. He learnt what it meant, in the practical essentials, to be a commando officer; he learnt how to handle the latest military weapons, the layout of current assault courses, how to read and send Morse and semaphore signals, how to change a guard. . . . He learnt military regulations, he learnt practical regimental etiquette, he learnt to drive a tank, he learnt to inspect a company of men. . . . Practical was the watchword; the emphasis was on the essential skills of his supposed background with which books wouldn't be able to help him.

He had had just the one week; and at the end of it the expert instructors who had dealt with him had confessed themselves astounded to a man.

But he knew he still had a long way to go.

He had slightly less of a long way to go by the time Ruth Barnaby came for her second visit. He told her about Rockham's surprise appearance.

"For a moment," he confessed, "I was almost tempted by his offer to get me out."

"You should have agreed," she said at once. "There'd certainly have been no doubt about his finding your escape convincing if he'd engineered it himself."

Simon looked at her soberly.

"There would have been just one little problem with that,

though," he pointed out. "What about the half dozen or so warders who might have been mown down as a by-product of Rocky-boy's rescue swoop?"

Ruth made an impatient dismissive gesture.

"I'm sure that could have been avoided somehow."

"But how?" he said practically. "He'd have no good reason to confide the details of the whole plan to me. In fact, he'd 've been a fool if he did, since I just might have decided to earn myself some nice safe remission by double-crossing him. And if he hadn't given me all the dope, including exactly how and when I was to be spirited away, I wouldn't have been in any position to get warnings to sundry people who'd otherwise be candidates for becoming sundry corpses."

"But Bert Nobbins would probably have been in the picture," the girl said. "Or, at least, enough to give us some inkling of when and how you'd be sprung."

In the short silence that ensued, Simon Templar experienced a sinking sensation which was closely connected with a growing conviction that he was not entirely in command of the situation.

"And who the blue blazes," he inquired in a voice heavy with restraint, "is Bert Nobbins?"

"Their Paymaster," she said. "He's also one of ours. Pelton put him in as a back-up for Randall. But he's not the type to step into Randall's place. Pelton says you're to ignore him."

CHAPTER 5

Those last few days had certainly dragged. For a while, after Ruth's second visit, Simon had fumed at having been kept in the dark about Pelton's opportunist catapulting of the hitherto desk-bound Nobbins into The Squad as Paymaster when the vacancy had providentially arisen only weeks before. But then he had given up fuming, had sat down to do some thinking which at least began to encompass the new factor that now had to be reckoned with, revised his assessment of Pelton again, and finally gone back to his books and notes. And slowly those last few days had ticked away . . . until three were left . . . then two . . .

Then one: and with the recurrence of Gascott's convenient malaria he had been moved to the prison wards.

Without digressing too far into the details of the plan that had been worked out, it may reasonably be disclosed that on the following day a certain vehicle arrived to make a delivery of medical supplies, and that when it was driven out through the prison gates again the dark moustached man at the wheel was not the same dark moustached man who had driven it in.

Within two hours Simon Templar was on his way to Peters-field, skimming the big cream-and-red Hirondel down the Portsmouth Road with even more inner zest than usual and only a shade less outward élan. He was still savouring the incomparable blessed wine of recovered freedom, and fighting a powerful impulse to scamper and frolic about maniacally in the sweet open air like a puppy let out for a run. But a degree of inconspicuousness seemed called for; and scampering, he judged, might have attracted some attention.

The hue and cry was out for Gascott—and genuinely. Rockham's possible accomplices in the various arms of the official establishment being an unknown factor, only the absolutely essential minimum of reliable stalwarts among prison and police staff had been told the truth about their now absquatulated detainee. The rest of them were playing it for real. And that was emphatically the way Simon Templar preferred it, even though it did mean that every village bobby in the land would be on the lookout for him.

Ruth Barnaby met him in the late afternoon at Petersfield, arranged garaging of his car, and drove him the last few miles in her own sporty two-seater.

The Bull at Kyleham was a comfortable inn, and handily placed just under a mile from the wall surrounding Rockham's fifty-five-acre base, which she pointed out to him as they passed it. The publican was a harmless soul whose cooperation had been easily enough ensured by a bit of official, not to say officious, finger-to-the-lips confidentiality. He had been told, in other words, only what he absolutely had to know; which was that for reasons having to do with national security he would kindly look no further for a relief barmaid than the attractive and competent-seeming young woman who was introduced to him as, simply, Ruth. As instructed, he provided her with a room and asked no questions; and in return she ably performed her duties behind the bar. It was as simple as that.

It was, technically, just a few minutes before opening time, so there was no one else in the bar when they came in.

"What can I get you?" she asked.

"A pint of Guinness for a start," he said. "Just to rinse the dust off the tonsils."

She went behind the bar and drew it. The Saint took a long and appreciative pull at the brimming tankard, and settled himself on a stool.

"Freedom," he declared expansively to his audience of one, "is a thing you never truly value till after you've been deprived of it. Which I suppose puts it squarely in the same bracket as just about anything else in the world that's worth having."

The girl set down a glass she had been vigorously drying—and so brought to an end, for the time being, an entertainment which owed a lot to her natural endowments and also something to the well-fitting sweater that inadequately concealed them.

"Prison seems to have brought out the philosopher in you," she observed.

"I suppose," he said, "that to anyone who ever did a stretch in Buchenwald, or in an old-fashioned English public school—to paraphrase one of our more eminent *literati*—Brixton would have seemed like a home away from home."

Ruth Barnaby reached down for a well-fitted haversack which she had brought in with her, and put it on the counter in front of him.

She said: "Here's the stuff you asked for."

Simon picked it up. It was light for its size. He opened it and took out two bulging oilskin bags. In the bottom of the haversack he could see a lightweight nylon rope ladder of the special design he had stipulated.

He peered into one of the oilskin bags, poking around in it with a lean brown hand, and nodded approvingly.

"The other one's the same?" he inquired.

"Identical. Just as you asked. That's three ladders altogether, and two of everything else." She dipped into her handbag and brought out a large manilla envelope. Rapidly she pointed to each item of the contents which she drew half out of it. "Local maps, aerial photo of Kyleham House Estate, details of guard patrols . . . and all Bert Nobbins's reports. All two of them," she added with a hint of malicious satisfaction.

The Saint looked at his watch and stood up.

"Thanks. I think I'll take these as my cue to withdraw to your back room," he said good-humouredly. He finished his pint, and picked up the folder and haversack. "A public bar's just a bit too public for serious study—and any minute now your regulars are going to be piling through the door in droves, tongues hanging out. See you later."

He had often had occasion to dilate satirically upon the parlous state of a nation whose idiotic nanny-like licensing laws frowned on the thirst of its citizens except within prescribed periods of the day. But just now he had more pressing matters to attend to, and he gave them his undivided concentration for the next two hours.

When the girl came through to the back room after that interval, he had already buttoned up his dark raincoat and shouldered the haversack.

"I'm on my way," he said. "It'll be dark enough by the time I get to the merry old health farm."

"Good luck," she said, almost perfunctorily.

"I'll try to give you the first news about o-two-hundred hours," he said. "Be outside the wall, about fifty yards east of the main gate. Okay?"

He picked up the single grip bag that was his luggage, went out by the back door, and melted into the dark.

There was a quarter-moon and a light mist, a blend of visibility and cover that suited the Saint's immediate purpose very well. It took him less than twenty minutes to reach Kyleham House, and he smiled with a grim mirthless satisfaction as he saw the wall ten feet high, looming up blankly out of the mist.

This was what the weeks of preparation had been all about. Behind that wall, and three hundred yards beyond the electrified inner fence, he would find John Rockham and The Squad—just as Jack Randall must have found them, on the sortie that was to be the last he ever made.

The Saint's jaw tightened as he swung the grip case in under the shadow of the wall and opened the haversack.

Among the useful articles it contained was a rope ladder made of the thinnest possible parachute cord that would support a man's weight; it was no more than six feet long, and had a big U-shaped claw of tempered steel attached to one end. He had to throw the grappling-iron up to hook over the top of the wall, in which he succeeded at the second attempt, and then to scale the ladder was only a matter of moments.

He paused briefly astride the wall, assuring himself that all was clear on the other side, before repositioning the ladder for his descent and eventual return.

The fence was only three yards beyond; he could see it clearly in the subdued moonlight: the solid wooden posts at eight-foot intervals, and stretched between them the thick continuous copper wires running parallel, about nine inches apart—the top one a good seven feet high.

An Olympic high-jumper might have cleared it, with a good run and at some hazard to his marriageability; but it would have been impossible to climb over it or through it without touching the wires and absorbing whatever unpleasant voltage they carried.

The surgical operation which the Saint performed on this obstacle was simple enough in principle, and he could easily have applied it to all the strands in the section of the fence which was his patient. But that would have taken quite a bit longer; and anyway with reasonable care he would be able to manage his subsequent excursions satisfactorily with just the bottom wire neutralized, leaving a safe eighteen-inch height to squirm under. Beside which, there would be less danger of his scalpel work being discovered.

That was one calculated risk.

He had to do his doctoring by the little natural light that happened to be available. This consisted of connecting a heavily insulated length of wire from his haversack to the lowest electrified strand, at the post, leading it across through the thick grass to the next post, and up that post again to reconnect with the same strand. Having thus bridged the distance between the posts—in case an alarm would have been set off if the original circuit had been crudely broken—he was able to excise the bypassed wire, using a special pair of nonconductive cutters which were included in the equipment he had requisitioned.

As a finishing touch, he fastened a length of string between the fence posts at the same level, to make the gap in the wire less obvious.

He knew that any really close scrutiny would be bound to reveal the substitution, but he just had to bank on the likelihood that a fence more than a mile long wouldn't regularly get a yard-by-yard inspection.

By taking sight bearings on a couple of trips inside the grounds, he made sure of being able to locate his handiwork again without hesitation, and then returned to the road outside as he had come, after hiding the haversack and some of its equipment under a bush beside the fence.

A few minutes later he was outside the main entrance.

The gates were of heavy wrought iron, massively bolted and locked. Beside a small brass plate bearing the words

THE PHYSICAL EFFICIENCY CENTRE

there was a bell-push. He leaned on it for a few seconds. He could see a light in the gate lodge, and presently two athletic-looking men emerged. They were dressed alike, in dark-blue denims and black roll-neck pullovers. One man was carrying a powerful torch, which he shone full in the Saint's face. The other man kept one hand behind his back, and it didn't take a clairvoyant to guess what might be in it.

"Name?" demanded a surly voice from behind the lantern.

"Simon Templar," said the Saint in Gascott's rasping voice.

CHAPTER 6

It was an outrageous flourish of the kind he couldn't resist. And as a variant of the effective technique of deception by the obvious, it had a potential practical function, too. A George Gascott who had announced himself under another name, especially if by doing so he was making the ridiculous claim to be the Saint, was less likely to be suspected at some point of being actually a phoney.

The surly voice said: "Come again?"

"Simon Templar," he repeated. "Tell Rockham I've come to sew him a few mailbags."

There was silence for a few moments as the two guards absorbed this revelation. Their impulse, he knew, was to reject it outright—which might have been unfortunate for him, since their method of rejection would probably have contained no milk of human kindness. But he could see them wavering with uncertainty.

The spokesman spoke again.

"Wait there."

He went back into the gate lodge, leaving his partner standing on silent watch, and Simon amused himself by imagining the exact course of the conversation on the phone with Rockham, whom he was confident would add it up in two seconds flat.

And he was right. A minute later the character with the torch re-emerged. He had a jangling bunch of keys in the other hand.

"Mr. Gascott, is it?" he said with rather less surliness and rather more respect in his voice.

Gascott had an arrogant way of half-inclining his head in a confirming gesture that was barely on the affirmative side of indifference. The Saint produced just that condescending wag of the head now, and to perfection, so that any impulse to amiable conversation that might have been about to burgeon was nipped firmly in the bud till after he had opened the heavy gates enough to let the Saint through, and had slammed the bolts and padlocks back into place.

Then the gatekeeper said: "There'll be a jeep for you in a minute"; and in about that time Simon heard the note of an engine puttering through the mist, and saw the twin cones of light sweeping down the long curve of driveway from the main buildings.

He climbed into the jeep beside the driver; the man nodded to him and grunted a greeting. He was dressed like the two guards, and he had a revolver on the parcel shelf, within easy reach of his right hand.

As the jeep backed and turned, Simon automatically registered and memorised the layout of the front entrance and the gatehouse and driveway. Almost as soon as they had moved off again in forward gear, they passed through a gap which was probably the one single breach in the whole length of the engirdling electrified fence—or had been, until his preparatory forays over the wall.

The main buildings were an architectural hotchpotch spanning two and a half centuries. The original Kyleham House had been one of the county's principal manor houses. Successive owners, presumably increasingly plutocratic and insensitive, had added wing after unbefitting wing, and piled annexe upon incongruous annexe; and during its days as a boarding college, still more extensions and new outbuildings had further compounded the desecration, so that the whole effect was almost of a random assemblage that a child might have made with a lot of dull-coloured play-bricks of ill-assorted shapes and sizes.

At the centre of the sprawl of buildings, embedded in the larger structure that had grown by accretion, was the original manor house, preserved virtually unaltered. Its façade was elegant, white-painted, colonnaded. The jeep stopped in front of it, and the driver led Simon in through the main door and up a curved staircase that must have been designed with the house itself.

The driver opened a door leading off the landing and announced laconically: "This is him."

He went away, and the Saint saw that he had been shown into a sort of anteroom. There was a door at the far end—leading, he guessed, to Rockham's office—and there were two men seated in the room. They were dressed like the others except that their pullovers were grey.

The two faces that turned towards him belonged to the men he would shortly know as Lembick and Cawber; and if those faces were lit up with openhearted friendliness it must have been by bulbs of micro-wattage.

"Good evening, boys," the Saint rasped. He held up a restraining hand to stem the nonexistent flow of conversation. "Wait. Don't tell me. Let me guess. That must be the Head's office." He pointed at the farther door. "And you"—he beamed at them—"you must be a couple of naughty boys waiting for six of the best. You really must stop this smoking in the lavatory, you know."

He laughed in that hollow way; and the chunky transatlantic half of the welcoming party lumbered off his chair and looked at him aslant.

"So you're Gascott, huh? And you said you was Simon Templar —the Saint! A comedian. You notice that, Lembick?" He kept his eyes fixed on the Saint while addressing the other man. "You notice that? He's a funnyman."

Simon put a hand to his mouth, yawned elaborately, and gazed idly around at the ceiling, while the other half of the welcoming party, which rapidly established itself as Caledonian, said:

"We'll have some fun with him then—won't we, Cawber?" There was a hard edge of sadistic anticipation in the crag-faced Lembick's voice. To Simon he said fiercely: "Ye'll train under us!"

"Och, laddie!" Simon exclaimed in an appalling parody of Lembick's accent. "I cannae wait! But what d'ye have in mind tae teach me? Wuid it be tossing the caber? Or wuid ye prefairrr tae instrrruct me in the proper care and feeding of the domestic sporrran?"

Abruptly he strode to Rockham's door; he knocked once and was on his way in even before the monosyllable "Come!" had snapped its way through the air, and before Lembick and Cawber had realised what was happening.

They followed indignantly in his wake.

"Boss—he just barged right past us . . ." Cawber trailed off, glaring at the Saint; and Rockham waved him down placatingly.

"Never mind, Cawber. Mister Gascott's a very positive personality. That's why I wanted him to join us."

The pale blue eyes appraised the Saint in this new setting; and the Saint returned the compliment, looking at Rockham and Rockham's office with a frank evaluative openness that betokened complete and calm self-confidence. Behind him, in contrast, Lembick and Cawber shifted awkwardly on their feet, exactly like the errant schoolboys which he had twitted them for resembling.

Rockham's office might have been—perhaps had been—designed to make men like Lembick and Cawber feel acutely ill at ease. A luxurious thick-piled carpet in a dark classical design blended perfectly with quietly decorous furniture of—the Saint guessed—the eighteenth century. Against this restrained background, the effect of a huge shock-colour abstract on one wall was electrifying.

Without being too fanciful or pseudopsychologically analytical, he mused, you could see that room as symbolising two poles of civilisation. On the one hand, culture; and on the other, violence, or naked power. And they met and clashed in that room just as they met and clashed in the man himself.

Rockham was clearly a very deliberate sophisticate. The cultivated exterior was like a hard but semitransparent coat of varnish that did little to hide the man's essential ruthlessness. Simon Templar had broken a lance with most of the available varieties of assorted villains in his time; and his highly attuned antennae told him beyond doubt that Rockham was as formidable as any of the species.

"Take a seat," Rockham said, ignoring his two standing subordinates. "A glass of port?"

"Very civil of you."

Rockham got up from his leather-trimmed roll-top desk and strolled over to a corner cabinet. He was wearing a perfectly cut dove-grey lounge suit.

"Congratulations on the breakout," he said as he poured the two drinks. "You certainly didn't waste much time."

"I didn't much care for the diet. Or the view."

Rockham's big square jaw creased momentarily in a mirthless smile as he handed Simon a glass.

"You came straight here."

It was a calm statement, containing neither surprise nor inquiry; yet somehow it demanded an answer.

"As soon as I could." Simon decided that he could afford to temper Gascott's unpleasanter style for the moment, and he consciously blunted the sharp edge of arrogance in his manner. "After all," he said, "I have to hide out somewhere. And you were right— I need the spondulicks. Three thousand a month, I think you said."

"Two." Rockham corrected him impassively; but even the lower figure had a discernible stiffening effect on Lembick and Cawber, and the Saint could practically hear their hostility crackling like static in the air.

He made a sour face, and then permitted himself a grin.

"A pity," he said wistfully. "Still, I suppose one must try to put up with life's small inconveniences. Man was born to suffer, so they say." He held the glass up to the light and twirled it approvingly by its elegant spirated stem. "Unusual shape for Waterford."

"Specially designed for De Valera," Rockham confided, looking gratified at the appreciation. "What do you make of the port?"

Simon wafted the glass contemplatively back and forth beneath his nostrils for a moment, and then sipped and savoured it.

"Taylor twelve," he pronounced. "Quite a favourite of mine, as it happens."

There was a sudden hiss of pent-up exasperation from Lembick.

"Aye," he scowled. "That's all very fine. But d'ye know a weapon like you know that stuff?"

He dragged a pistol from his pocket and sent it spinning hard at the Saint, who caught it adroitly with his left hand, putting his drink down at the same moment with his right.

"Walther PPK, 7.65 millimetres," he commented with professional detachment. "A good general-purpose weapon."

He seemed hardly to look at the gun, yet in a few deft movements he had extracted the magazine and cleared the breech, and proceeded with further dismantling. As he stripped down the gun he sent the parts, beginning with the magazine, flying in quick succession at Lembick, who fielded them awkwardly.

"As I say, a nice little weapon," the Saint rasped as he flipped the last piece—the heavy butt section—at Lembick's midriff.

Rockham smiled broadly at the exhibition.

"Satisfied, Lembick?"

"We'll see," grunted the lowering Lembick. "We'll see how he makes out in training."

To Simon, Rockham said: "I'm impressed with you, Gascott. But don't get any ideas above your present station. You'll be watched closely. You won't be permitted to leave the premises unaccompanied—not until I'm personally satisfied of your bona fides."

"Confined to barracks?" Simon shrugged unconcernedly. "Suits me, for the time being. I'm not exactly anxious to go on public parade just at the moment."

The other nodded, toying thoughtfully with his glass.

"I think there's a future for you in The Squad. I hope you'll think so too, when you've seen how we operate. Tomorrow you'll be shown our facilities."

"For the . . . cultivation of physical efficiency?" The Saint's infinitesimal lift of one eyebrow was only faintly mocking.

Rockham chuckled.

"A neat cover, don't you think?"

"Good enough to explain anything a visiting meter reader might see, I guess."

"Exactly. We have to let a few outsiders in. Deliveries, phone repairs, and so forth. The physical efficiency idea covers the lot: the fit men, the gunshots—we've got a pistol and a rifle range— the exercises, of one kind and another."

Simon looked into the blue eyes that were almost transparently pale; and he saw that those eyes burned with a kind of cold fire of pride, and he knew then that John Rockham was separated by only a hair's breadth from madness.

"What about passers-by who see your sign," he inquired, "and feel an overpowering urge to get themselves physically efficient?"

"I simply turn them away," Rockham said, smiling and spreading his hands in a gesture that conveyed how effortlessly he was able to put prospective customers off. "We're always full. We're a very *exclusive* establishment."

And Rockham laughed, and the Saint knew that there was no more mirth in that laugh than in the hollow one he himself had perfected for his role.

The laugh, the smile, faded. Rockham's manner became instantly brisk and businesslike.

"We're flexibly organised here," he said. "No fixed ranks—except mine as C in C. I assign authority for the duration of each individual mission. Lembick and Cawber here, as you'll have gathered, have special duties in training and generally keeping an eye on new recruits. They have my authority to drive you, and drive you hard." Rockham stood up. "I'll admit there have been one or two unfortunate errors of recruitment—men who couldn't make the grade. It's a pity about them. We've no room for slackers or failures in The Squad." He shook Simon by the hand. "But somehow I don't expect you to be among them. I expect great things of you, Gascott."

To Lembick and Cawber he said: "Show him his room." And as they followed the Saint through the door, he added quietly, "You've got a week to bring him up to scratch."

CHAPTER 7

The Saint woke up from his light doze at one o'clock in the morning with that infallible catlike faculty for instant alertness which had served him so well in his hazardous career.

But this time it was not that his ever-vigilant hearing had roused him in response to some faint intrusion of real sound. It was simply that his mental alarm clock, a wholly inaudible and discreet device which he had set a couple of hours earlier, had gone off exactly as intended. He had told it to wake him up at one; and it had done so.

Timing was of some importance if he was to avoid risking an encounter with the guard patrols. Their concern was chiefly with any unauthorised visitors, but his own position if he were intercepted would be no more healthy.

The estate was roughly rectangular, with the conglomeration of buildings somewhat west of centre and with the main gate set in the middle of the long south wall. From the window of his room he could see the two-man inner patrol during part of their continuous circuit around the buildings, and he knew that there was a similar patrol throughout the night on the much wider circuit just inside the wall. Pelton had mentioned guard dogs, but he had not yet seen any sign of them—perhaps they were kept in reserve, to be unleashed only in extreme emergency.

The three-storey block he was in stood a little apart from the monstrosity of a central building. It was a comparatively recent structure, built in the days of the college to house the privileged senior pupils in study-bedrooms. Simon's was one of some fifty such rooms, identically small and opening identically off L-shaped corridors on each floor, along with the "usual offices."

He was one floor up, and counted it a minor advantage that his room was next door to a "usual office."

He got out of the narrow bed and arranged the clothing he had arrived with, and one of the two pillows, to make it look as though he might still be in it. He didn't know how far Lembick and Cawber's brief to keep an eye on him went, or whether it included making close checks in the middle of the night, but that was another chance he just had to take.

He put on the regulation denims, plimsolls, and black pullover he had been issued with earlier after his own things had been thoroughly searched, and went noiselessly into the corridor and into the bathroom on the other side, which overlooked the direction he wanted to take through the grounds. Outside its window was a convenient drainpipe, of obviously solid vintage, which combined with more ancient ivy to give him an easy ladder to the neglected flower bed below.

Approximately as a leopard glides through tangled jungle undergrowth with both speed and uncanny silence, so Simon Templar transferred himself from there to his chosen spot near the south east corner of the wall.

The analogy is only approximate, because admittedly he had no creeping lianas or other dense vegetative hindrances to contend with. Most of the estate was open land; though there were a few sparsely wooded areas and he had to pass through one of these in the course of his 250-yard sortie.

Near the far edge of this spinney, he waited for two or three minutes till he heard the footsteps of the outer patrol as they turned to skirt the wall. They were on time to the minute; and if they kept to schedule it would be three-quarters of an hour before they came around again.

He emerged from the tenebrous dark just short of the section of fence which, thanks to his earlier preparatory work, would hardly detain him at all. But first, after removing the piece of string with which he had replaced the bottom wire, he reached through and brought out the haversack from under the bush where he had hidden it, and took out a one-piece oversuit, which had been packed into a remarkably small space. He put it on. It was dark grey and made of a thin but tough canvaslike material, and it covered and protected every square inch of his clothing—and the leggings even terminated in overshoes, made out of extra thicknesses of the same tough material.

Then he crawled safely through the space he had previously created, under what had now become the lowest of the live wires.

Extracting his rope ladder from under his clothing, he succeeded this time in hooking it over the top of the wall at the first attempt. In a few seconds more, he landed lightly outside the wall and looked around. A few yards away, an unlit parked car faced him. He glided like a wraith towards it, keeping close in under the shadow of the wall until he was sure the car was Ruth Barnaby's, and that it was Ruth Barnaby who was sitting behind the wheel.

He drummed a spirited tattoo on the roof and got in beside her.

"Doesn't the romper suit make me look fetching?" he said. "I feel a bit like a truant from the nursery. Except that this playpen has twelve-foot walls, and nannies about as kindly and maternal and lovable as any rattlesnake with a sore tail."

Faithful readers who have come to expect that the female lead will invariably be captivated by Simon Templar's bantering charm and piratical good looks will now need to come to terms with harsh reality, which is that, incredible as it may seem, not every woman found the Saint irresistible. Just occasionally he encountered one who seemed peculiarly blind to his dazzling virtues, and almost deaf to his brilliant persiflage.

This might have been because of the mysterious chemistry of personality whereby two people, when mixed and shaken, sometimes precipitate an immediate curd of mutual antipathy. The Saint preferred to like people if he possibly could, but he had to admit that the psychic factor was real enough. Or it might be because the female in question was so besotted at the time with some other male that she was temporarily in a condition indistinguishable from imbecility. Simon Templar didn't present the problem to himself in so many words, but he did notice.

Although he wasn't aware of any actual antagonism on either side, it seemed like damned hard work to pierce through Ruth Barnaby's professional single-mindedness to anything softer or lighter-hearted underneath.

"It does the job, though?" she inquired dispassionately, indicating the oversuit.

"It does," he said. "It keeps my clothes from getting dirty and scuffed or muddy on an outing like this and saves awkward questions about where I've been and what I've been doing."

"I can tell Pelton that you're well and truly installed, then?"

"Yes. Though I've nothing to report as yet. But by the way, you never did explain how Nobbins has been reporting."

"He didn't—not till he became a trusty. Trusties are allowed odd days off. But that wasn't till he'd been there a couple of weeks or so. And then he sent those reports you read."

"And they weren't too helpful. I suppose he wouldn't have been up to climbing walls?"

"Neither physically nor psychologically," she said. "He's been scared stiff ever since he went in."

"Then why *did* he go in?"

She shrugged.

"Pelton's idea. Bert had been griping a bit about always being behind the scenes—you know, the poor grey anonymous little man. Pelton wanted someone else on the inside in a hurry. He didn't want to risk sending in another frontline agent. The face just might have been recognised. And then this vacancy came up. Randall found out that Rockham needed somebody to do his accounts, look after the men's pay, keep records—all that sort of thing."

"And Nobbins had the right qualifications?"

"For that, yes—he used to be in the Pay Corps. But for active service as an infiltrator, no—in my opinion."

The outline facts weren't new to the Saint at this point. But for the first time he was beginning to see what Bert Nobbins's real position in the affair might be; and that dawning realisation, or suspicion, made the hairs on the back of his neck stand up and do what felt like an icy little minuet.

"But Pelton put him in regardless," he said slowly.

"It was a risk," she admitted, without saying for whom. "But without Bert's contribution it would have been a lot harder to brief you for your job. And he was keen to prove himself outside his own field."

"Which is?"

"Information handling," the girl said. "That's analysis of in-coming reports. For example, from Resident Directors—you know the set-up overseas. Deciphering, extraction, collating, condensing. It's mostly dull, boring, routine work. But Bert's good at it. I know—I worked under him for a couple of years."

Thoughts were chasing each other around in the Saint's head like wasps in a jam jar. Somewhere in this whole set-up was some-thing—or maybe it was two or three or four things—that didn't fit no matter which way up you turned it and no matter what angle you looked at it from. His nose for these matters told him only one thing for certain: somewhere, in some way that it was beyond his present knowledge and understanding to discern, the game was rigged.

It was a little like being in a room where any of the angles or perspectives might be individually possible but which made an im-possible whole, so that you felt a weirdly subtle vertigo. The sort of room certain psychological researchers have managed to create to test the disorienting effects of visual incoherence.

And who were the people who formed the corners of this partic-ular psychological test chamber?

Rockham. Pelton. Ruth Barnaby. Gascott. The Saint himself. Nobbins. Jack Randall. . . .

Jack Randall.

She had said, just now, that Pelton hadn't wanted to risk *send-ing in another frontline agent.*

That might have been just an imprecision of speech on her part.

Or it might mean something the thought of which made the Saint grit his teeth in premonition.

"What made Randall do a damn-fool thing like going in on his own to look at The Squad, without a cover?" he asked bluntly.

She looked at him in surprise.

"Orders, of course," she said. "Pelton told him to."

CHAPTER 8

It was a still-angry Simon Templar who went back to his room shortly after by an exact reversal of his outward route with its incidental manoeuvres, except for leaving the rope ladder under the bush by the fence, for future use and to safeguard it from being found in any search of his room.

The excursion had taken up little more than half an hour; but in consequence of it he was plunged into continuous if not very productive thought for twice as long again.

It was the sort of session in which, once, he would have smoked and enjoyed one cigarette after another: and several times in the course of that hour he found himself wishing heartily that his chronicler's nicotine-stained conscience hadn't insisted, some time back, on the Saint's following his own example and giving the habit up.

At an obscenely early hour of the morning, Cawber appeared, and took his new charge, with a distinct lack of outward brotherly love, to breakfast in the big hall which had been the school refectory.

Cawber, the Saint decided, was a man nobody could ever have described as chummy.

They were joined by Leander—not someone either whom he would ever have been tempted to take to his bosom.

But then, if the two of them were unpleasant specimens, he could be just as unpleasant himself, in the person of Gascott. He knew that he had worked himself so thoroughly into the part by now that on a superficial level he could give as good—or as bad— as he got when it came to the sort of sadistic bullying in which these two transplanted drill sergeants evidently specialised.

There was a man called Ungill at the next breakfast table

whom Simon had vaguely noticed in Brixton. Ungill had left a week or more before him, and a lot more officially. They nodded to each other now. What amazed the Saint was the evident decline in Ungill's health. He looked exhausted and ill. His skin was the colour of pale cheddar; he seemed to be in a state of quivering nervous tension, and he hobbled painfully to the table and lowered himself into the chair with obvious difficulty.

"Got a little pain, have we, Ungill?" Lembick leered. "Don't you worry—we'll soon get that sorted out for you. A nice brisk little five-mile run with the pack on and you'll be as right as rain. Or maybe you'd prefer an hour or two's wrestling with Cawber. You know how he enjoys that!"

Cawber licked his lips. There were flecks of cornflake on them, but Simon had the feeling he would have licked them anyway.

"Yeah," he grinned. "Lemme have him!"

Ungill's complexion went a couple of shades paler.

"Please, Lembick," he whined. "Couldn't I give training a miss today. My back—"

"Your back my backside!" Lembick cut in sneeringly. You'll not shirk while I've anything to do with it. And stop your snivelling and cringing—you make me sick!" With the air of a judge passing sentence and enjoying it, he added: "Cawber's going to be busy with me, inducting the new man here. You'll do the five-mile run—with a fifty-pound pack. Twenty times around the big field."

Ungill, the Saint knew, was a pretty tough egg by ordinary standards. He was old lag, and fairly typical of the breed in most ways. He wasn't old in years—he was maybe in his mid-thirties—so much as in prison experience, having been in and out of penal institutions of one kind and another from the age of twelve. In recent years he had specialised, when he wasn't actually paying the penalty for his specialisation, in keeping up with the people whose job it was to build bigger and better safes; which he did by devising bigger and better methods of blasting his way into them. And it was presumably for his expertise in explosives that Rockham had wanted him. Though at this rate, he didn't look like having him for much longer.

With Lembick and Cawber at least, the Saint reflected, it

would be a pleasure to exercise Gascott's sarcastically contemptuous tongue. The only trouble was, they had a certain advantage, for the time being, in any debates that might develop, because he was supposed to knuckle under and obey their orders.

All things considered, he wasn't looking forward to the next week.

"How's your judo?" Lembick fired the question at him a little later, when they reached the drill hall, a vast hangarlike structure between the main house, which they had just left, and the block where the Saint's room was.

"Rusty," he replied untruthfully, gazing around at the scene of varied combative and callisthenic activity.

He counted five pairs of men practising judo, grunting and flurrying and thudding onto the huge canvas mat in one corner. Two pairs of men with boxing gloves, nearer to him, were sparring without pulling many punches. The area in another corner was laid out as a more or less conventional gym, with a horse, bars, rings, and the rest; and these facilities too were in full use.

"We believe in total physical fitness," Lembick commented, with a fanatical glint in his eye. "All this isn't for fun, or *sport*." He spat out the word with distaste. "A man—a soldier—has to be properly *fit*."

"We got a system here," Cawber put in. "For the first two weeks, you train. That means we get you fit, if you ain't already. And you won't be," he added, baring his ill-assorted teeth in what his mother might have called a smile. "And after we've gotten you fit, we keep you fit. We have a daily programme. Except when you're on assignments."

"In your case," Lembick said as they entered another building, "the training's going to be squeezed into one week instead of two. The boss seems to think you can take it. Today we'll start finding out if he's right."

"We're gonna have to work you twice as hard!" said Cawber with exaggerated relish.

They were in a small storage warehouse. The racks that lined the walls were piled up with a bewildering variety of military, police, and other uniforms that made the Saint catch his breath with amazement.

Lembick followed Simon's sweeping gaze.

"Nice, eh? You name it, we've got it. Naval ratings, police, U. S. Army, all ranks, plenty of British regimental stuff—including some Scottish regiments," he said with something as close to pride as that hard-edged voice could have come.

In the rest of his brief tour Simon was given a sight of everything in that same cursory way. The armaments store was a real eye-opener; and he quietly filed away what he had seen in his memory for future reference, at the same time noting that some of Pelton's figures were confirmed as questionable in the light of the racks upon racks of the latest military-issue weapons he had seen: gleaming new Lee-Enfield 303's, and Webley .38 revolvers, among other interesting items of more specialised issue.

And all the time, in the back of his mind, he was trying to form a hypothesis to explain the persistent sensation that he was a piece in a game he didn't fully understand.

Simon Templar's week of fitness training began.

He knew it would be tough—even for him. He knew he was already about as fit, about as general-purpose fit, as a man could be. He had always kept himself that way—not only because his active career demanded it, but also from a sheer zest for living, a zest which quite naturally included a real and enduring pleasure in the perfect functioning of hand and nerve and eye and muscle. And he had started out, he knew, with enviable physical assets. He had the kind of frame that yielded maximum power and speed in relation to its bulk. It is well known that bigger bodies are less efficient machines, other things being equal, than smaller ones, and it was well known to Simon Templar. Size for size, a flyweight Olympic weight lifter is a deal stronger than his more massive counterparts in the heavy divisions. Yet in life, he also knew, you were usually dealing with absolutes: on the whole, bigger men were stronger, and it was more important to be strong, period, than to be strong for your size.

The Saint was tall, but with not an ounce of surplus weight on his body. His reflexes were razor-sharp, which was another advantage that came partly from the dice game of heredity and partly from practice and habit. So he was as well equipped to face any

challenge to his agility and endurance as any man could have
been.

But he knew something else, too. He knew that there was general-purpose fitness, which he had, and there were also various
kinds of special-purpose fitness. A man could be in the peak of
condition as a boxer, say, but as soon as he tried pole-vaulting, or
some other activity out of his usual field, he'd find muscles aching
that he never knew he had.

Simon Templar couldn't have run the hundred yards in nine
seconds, but he could sprint creditably enough when the need
arose. Equally he could have run or jogged for mile after mile
without serious signs of distress, though he wouldn't have won the
marathon. But long hard runs, at pace, and with an increasing
weight of stones in the rucksack on his back, were something for
which it inevitably took a bit of time to develop the special-purpose fitness.

And until you did develop it, every muscle in your body, after a
certain time, felt as if some malefic little arsonist had been at
work at its centre; every limb seemed to be encased in concrete;
and every joint felt as if its bearings had seized.

The Saint, in addition to these discomforts and the comparable
ones of wrestling with Cawber, practising judo with Lembick, and
doing all kinds of exercises for hours at a time, had a strategic
problem to settle: how much he should hold his performance
back to something nearer the average? By shining too much he
might be inviting Lembick and Cawber to make things still
harder for him; on the other hand, they seemed to be spurred on
to higher slights of happy sadism by any show of weakness in their
charges—as witness the case of Ungill. None of the others were
having quite as much difficulty as that, but some were a good halfway to exhaustion by the Saint's second day: for some of them,
their eighth or ninth. And whenever any of them showed signs of
flagging, Lembick or Cawber would instantly pounce and make
still greater demands.

In the end the Saint compromised by doing a little less well
than he could have in the weighted runs and other noncombative
departments, and considerably less well than he could have in the
physical tussles with the two trainers, though just well enough not

to get hurt. If he had needed to, he could have taken either of them in any form of unarmed combat, but he judged that that would have been an affront which might have provoked them to some vicious form of revenge. Also, there could be an advantage in keeping his superiority a secret for the time being.

Rockham had chosen his two trainers well. They might be crude and uncultured, with no interest in the finer things of life, but they were tough and relentless slave drivers. Perfect, in other words, for what the Saint saw as the main object of that so-called training. It certainly wasn't to produce what Simon had represented to himself as special-purpose fitness, unless Rockham foresaw significant numbers of missions in which his troops would need to run long distances wearing rock-filled or otherwise weighted rucksacks. It was simply to put new recruits to the test: a tough test that got down to the guts of a man, that took him again and again to the point of physical exhaustion or nausea, whichever came first; that drove him on to find more in reserve, another ounce of effort, when he thought he had been emptied of it all. And this against the continual goading and taunting and beating—sometimes literally—by those two despots of the drill-hall. It was make or break.

To survive in The Squad, you first had to survive Lembick and Cawber's tender ministrations.

Certainly Albert Nobbins would never have come through; Simon felt sure of that when he met him, on the second day. But the few noncombat staff, luckily for them, were exempted from the process.

By the morning of his sixth day, the Saint's resilient system had adapted completely to the physical slog—even though his beauty sleep had again been interrupted for a silent excursion over the wall to give Ruth Barnaby what small crumbs of useful new information he had been able to gather. She asked about missions, dates, plans; and he had to tell her that he still knew practically nothing. Missions simply weren't discussed beforehand except with the men who were to take part. And even supposing the Saint could have found one prepared to engage in casually indiscreet conversation, his own schedule while in training just wouldn't have left room for it. Aside from what he had seen on his tour—and that added nothing to what Nobbins had already reported—there was hardly anything useful he could report.

Which is not to say that nothing happened.

A few things did.

To begin with, he met Nobbins.

It was a fairly unspectacular event, in view of their later connection. Nobbins raised his pink bespectacled face from his papers for an instant, looked vaguely at Simon, murmured "How do you do?" politely, and that was the end of that. There was not even the smallest wisp of a flicker of anything that anyone might have taken as acknowledgement of a fellow infiltrator. Which confirmed that he had not been told the true identity of Gascott's impersonator.

That was a decision of Pelton's which the Saint approved of. Nobbins's cover in the name of Mike Argyle had been cobbled together in less that a week, and was liable to wear through at any moment. And Nobbins would not be likely to withstand the sort of pressure that could be put on him if he were caught. He might easily be forced to unburden himself of everything he knew. In which event the Saint much preferred that the role of Gascott wasn't included in that knowledge.

Another thing that happened during the first four days was that Ungill's performance fell steadily even further behind, and the castigations of him by Lembick and Cawber grew more raucous and savage.

"You're a disgrace, Ungill—a disgrace to The Squad!" Lembick yelled at him on the third day, his features set in livid fury, as Ungill tripped exhausted on the fourth consecutive round of the obstacle course. "You let me down in front of the new man. You've been working under me for ten days. He's been here three. And look at him!" He used the swagger stick he sometimes carried to point at the Saint, who looked fresh and unhurried; and then he belaboured Ungill across the shoulders with it. "A disgrace, Ungill! D'ye know what you're heading for?"

"Quitter classification, that's what," supplied the other member of the training duo in his Bronx twang. "And you know what happens when you're classified a quitter!"

And on the day after that Ungill wasn't seen at breakfast.

Nor again.

The Saint, who had advised him to give up and get out, inquired what had happened to him—hoping he had taken the advice and asked to be discharged. But Lembick and Cawber grinned evilly, and Cawber said:

"He decided to take a holiday. A real long one."

Exit Ungill.

Maybe he had asked for it, as maybe anyone did who joined that organisation without having his eyes tightly closed. But the Saint couldn't help feeling that this was one recruit who had lacked not only the physical stamina but also the vicious streak that service with The Squad demanded; and he mentally added it to the tally of scores that he heartily hoped he would someday have the pleasure of settling with Lembick and Cawber.

The only relief from their physical persecution was given by the few training sessions that interrupted their sovereignty. Once, Rockham delivered a talk on the organisation—revealing little Simon didn't already know. Twice they were given some small-arms instruction, to him superfluous, of the "naming of parts" variety. And there was a short practice stint each day on the shooting-ranges, although that was supervised by that same tyrannical pair.

Even while he was heroically resisting a frequent impulse to reply to some of Lembick's acts of tyranny with a smashing fist, he was afraid that he wouldn't be able to resist indefinitely, and the question was how long he could avoid some kind of showdown.

It happened on that sixth morning.

The group had just finished a practice session with Lembick on the judo mat—a session in which Simon had been singled out for the privilege of being hurled repeatedly to the canvas, ostensibly to illustrate a throw from which it just happened to be almost impossible to break-fall painlessly.

And he was still hopping mad from his role as literal fall-guy when Lembick's eye turned to two black-handled dirks mounted on the wall in a letter-X shape.

Lembick took one of them down. He flipped it in the air and caught it.

"The Scottish dirk. Myself, I prefer the Gaelic name, the *sgian dubh*." It sounded like "skee-an due" as he pronounced it. "The black knife. For close combat one of the finest weapons ever."

His flinty eyes roamed over the faces of the group, and stopped where he had already decided they would stop—at Simon Templar.

He pointed.

"You. Gascott. Now, I want you to come at me. No games, no holding back. Come hard."

He tossed the knife to Simon. Simon caught it by the handle. Lembick stood on the canvas mat a few yards in front of him, balanced easily on the balls of his feet, waiting.

The Saint said slowly: "There *could* be a nasty accident."

Lembick's eyes were like slits of Carborundum.

"I'm waiting for you, Gascott," he said intently.

Simon shrugged and edged forward across the mat towards him, aware of the audience.

Suddenly he made an overhand lunge—in less than deadly earnest, and knowing that it was not the attack of an expert knife fighter.

But Lembick wasn't pulling his own punches. He took a half-pace forward to meet the mock attack; and then the downward looping arc of the Saint's wrist was terminated abruptly and jarringly by the blocking V of a virtually impenetrable barrier formed by Lembick's crossed forearms. And then, without an instant's pause, one of those forearms smashed hard and sickeningly into the side of the Saint's neck.

He dropped the knife and for a moment he saw a fantasia of coloured lights that would have brought tears to the eyes of a firework display organiser. For a longer moment he heard a high-pitched buzzer singing in his ears like some demented gnat; and then as that sound died away he heard himself say, with an icy inclemency of purpose:

"I don't think I quite got that—laddie. Do you think we might try it once more?"

The challenge was unmistakable. Lembick's craggy features were impaled on two spear-points of frozen blue that were the Saint's eyes.

Lembick's lips curled back in a smile that was also a snarl.

"Pick it up, then." He indicated the knife. "And let's have you!"

Simon moved to the knife and bent down to pick it up, but that frosty impaling gaze never left Lembick's face.

And then the Saint came up off the floor like an uncoiling spring, and Lembick saw the upwards black-and-silver flash of the knife a fraction of a second too late.

Blood trickled from a gash in his left arm. And Simon Templar had already sprung back out of reach, after making that single well-judged slash.

"Was that closer to what you had in mind?" he asked coolly.

For a few seconds Lembick seemed uncomprehending as he stared at his bare arm with the trickle of blood running off it onto the canvas mat. And then something seemed to snap in him, and his eyes blazed with a sudden rage of realisation.

He flung himself at the wall and snatched down the second dirk, and whirled to face the Saint.

"You just made a bad mistake, Mister Gascott," he said through clenched teeth. "The *sgian dubh* is my weapon. I'm on my home ground!"

CHAPTER 9

There was total silence in the drill-hall except for the sound of quickened breathing from the two men circling each other warily, literally at daggers drawn. Another group who had been busy in the hall with a karate workout, chopping rhythmically away at planks of wood supported on bricks, stopped and joined the others as interested onlookers at the prospect of a fight.

At that moment the Saint was only dimly aware of them. For the present everything was blotted from the centre of his consciousness but his opponent and himself, circling grimly, each watching for a momentary relaxation of the other's alertness, and weighing the likely instant for a successful feint or lunge or slash with the knife.

The others had seen the tension building up over the past few days between Lembick and the supposed Gascott; and now they were watching it explode in that slow and potentially deadly tarantella, and their attention was riveted.

At some point Simon became peripherally aware that Rockham had come quietly in and was standing behind them.

But then abruptly the pattern changed. Lembick came racing at him in a kind of weaving charge, with the blade of the dirk slicing the air in arcs of flashing silver. But the Saint's anticipation was faster by a wafer-thin margin that allowed him to keep just a whisker beyond the reach of that blade, as he danced and swayed and bobbed—and waited.

That was the simple detached technique that he coolly and deliberately set out to apply. Lembick came after him, grunting and sweating and stabbing and slashing; and the Saint ducked and danced and sidestepped tirelessly, until there seemed to be an inescapable inevitability about the way that blade cleaved the air time after time, and never found its quicksilver target.

And then Lembick did what Simon was waiting for him to do. He overreached himself by the merest millimetre; but that was enough. Enough to create a momentary break in his balance which magnified the Saint's advantage in reaction time, to the point where he could bring his left hand down in a sizzling chop that thudded into Lembick's wrist joint.

The dirk went clattering and skittering off over the wood parquet floor beyond the edge of the mat, and with scarcely a pause Simon Templar sent his own weapon after it, to stick in the floor like a dart, so that both daggers came to rest blade to blade.

And then the Saint stood relaxed, with his arms at his sides. Yet even at that moment, when he was thinking of nothing except hitting Lembick as hard as he possibly could, habit ensured that he remembered to speak in Gascott's unpleasant rasp.

He said: "How good are you with bare knuckles, Lembick? I've been dying to find out. We're on *my* home ground now!"

And then he switched back into that same weaving, ducking, swaying mode of action again. But this time he went forward instead of back.

And there was every bit as much inevitability about his unstoppable attack as there had been in the elusiveness of his defence.

From Lembick's point of view, among all the myriad intersections of events and substantivities in time and space that an omniscient metaphysician might have recorded, the next few seconds contained only two configurative incidents of any significance. The first was when Simon Templar's left fist sank with piledriving power into the area about three inches below his sternum; and the second was when the Saint's other fist came scorching over his guard in a curving trajectory that terminated beside his chin.

The first blow would have been enough to keep an ordinary man writhing in winded agony for several minutes and hobbling thereafter. The second would have broken a jaw of less neanderthal solidity than Lembick's. Even on him their combined effect was spectacular enough. He sank to the floor with a glazed look in his eyes.

There was a silence in which Lembick's rough gasping breaths cut into the air like a coarse handsaw fighting through a tough log. Then Rockham stepped casually forward.

"I like your style, Gascott," he said. "And I like to see Lembick put in his place for once. I daresay he asked for it just now."

As he spoke—ignoring the writhing Lembick on the mat—he crossed to the plank the karate practisers had left in position, and he began pummelling it gently and rhythmically with the edges of his hands, gradually building up speed and power. "I know you've done well in getting back your old commando form. Tomorrow we'll consider you graduated. After that you'll have an assignment before long. Maybe very soon. . . . But until then, you and Lembick are going to have to live together as best you can. I don't want grudge fights carried on in The Squad."

Simon nodded.

"Anthropologists have lived with apes," he commented.

Rockham's two-handed tattoo on the thick plank was building up to a crescendo.

"Don't get *too* carried away, will you?" he said; and his manner was all smoothness and smiles and charm.

And then he smashed through the plank with one single culminating axe-like blow from his right hand, and strolled out urbanely without another glance at Lembick's still prostrate but now partly recovered form.

"*Na sir 's na seachainn an cath,*" said the Saint. "Neither seek nor shun the fight." And then for Lembick's benefit he added: "A girl from the Western Isles taught me a bit of Gaelic once."

He refrained from adding that that wasn't all she had taught him, or that the proverb had a wider significance for him right then than the obvious one.

Somehow, as he knew he would, he got through the rest of that day. Cawber worked the whole crew of them harder than ever, but studiously avoided picking on the Saint for special attention. To Simon, it was worth every bit of personal discomfort that Cawber could dish out to have had the satisfaction of putting down the American's co-tyrant, even at the cost of revealing perhaps too much of his own capabilities.

That night he had that incident to report, when he met Ruth, and one other thing.

"This evening," he told her, "Rockham had some visitors. Chinese or Japs, I'd guess. Four of them. They got out of a black Daimler, registration number GRD 4711."

Ruth delved into her bag for a notebook and jotted down the number.

"Thanks. Pelton'll be interested to hear *that*. Anything else?"

"Only that I didn't see our friend Nobbins, alias Argyle, all day. He certainly wasn't taking his meals."

"He's on leave again," the girl said. "Just for a couple of days. He's supposed to be having some dental work done. He reported to Pelton in London today."

The Saint frowned.

"You mean he went to Pelton's own office? Isn't that a bit crazy? Rockham's thoroughness might easily stretch to having Argyle-Nobbins watched during his little off-duty jaunts."

"It does," she said matter-of-factly. "There's a man on his tail the whole time. Bert's had to shake him off to get to Pelton."

The Saint looked at her from under dark brows that had arched into a questioning scepticism.

"And how does he manage that?"

She shrugged.

"There are various ways. You must know. Pelton gave him a few tips. There's the movies, for example. You can be through a side door and out while the watchdog's eyes are still getting used to the dark."

"Very clever," said the Saint sardonically. "And if a suspect deliberately and cunningly sheds his tail, doesn't that make him even more suspect?"

As he made his way silently back to his room, those words went oddly through his head again and again, like a refrain. "He reported to Pelton in London today."

And David Pelton was supposed to be the guiding genius of a highly sensitive operation . . .

In the morning he was considerably less than astounded when Rockham sent for him and Lembick and Cawber after breakfast, and revealed that the so-called Mike Argyle was under heavy suspicion.

"He may or may not have joined us under false pretences," Rockham said without emotion. "Some of the evidence points in that direction—and we can't afford to give him the benefit of what doubt there may be. So, as of yesterday, although he doesn't know it, Mister Argyle—ex-Captain Argyle, or whatever his real name may be—is no longer a member of The Squad. And as there is no such thing as an *ex*-member of our organisation . . ."

That was when Simon Templar was assigned to the job of executing Albert Nobbins—and he was to do it that same afternoon.

"It'll be your final test, and a decisive one," Rockham told him, while the two trainers glowered. "A sort of end-of-course exam, if you like. And if you do a good job, there's no limit to how far you can go with The Squad."

Somehow the Saint had to get word to Pelton, who would presumably know how to contact Nobbins-Argyle. But the Saint hadn't been given enough notice to report to Ruth Barnaby in the usual way.

On the schedule for the group of trainees that morning was the last and most punishing of their endurance tests—a six-mile cross-country race, with weighted packs, and with Cawber as whipper-in. When they were shown their course on the map beforehand, the Saint saw that they were due to pass right by the door of the Bull. And that might give him one slim chance of getting a warning to Ruth—and on to Nobbins.

When they set out there was a chill in the air that was exceptional even for that autumn. They were dressed in light track suits; yet Simon knew that before long, even in that amount of clothing, they would be steaming from their exertions. Each man carried thirty pounds of sand in the pack on his back. But the Saint knew that his own burden weighed substantially more. Cawber had seen to that, with a sly smirk of malevolence.

What he would have to do was to take a lead that would leave the rest of the field out of sight by the time he reached the Bull.

Simon Templar ran as he had never run before.

Steadily, inexorably, he drew farther and farther ahead of the others. Only Cawber could have kept up with him, since Cawber was running without a pack, but Cawber stayed at the rear of the party, where he could bully and chivvy the slowest with abuse or, if that failed, a well-aimed swipe of his swagger stick.

At first they followed a narrow rural lane, its yellowish unmetalled surface thumping to the tramp of their feet. Then after a little while they crossed a stile and struck off across rough pastureland; then uphill; then down through a chill dankish coniferous wood; then out across more open land, boggier than before; then along another stretch of country road; then more fields, and woods, and hills . . .

Two miles ground past under his pumping legs. Three miles; three and a half. At which point he was fully a quarter of a mile ahead of the next man—so that he was only occasionally within sight of any of the runners when for a few moments no bends or other obstacles intervened.

He was drenched in sweat; his back felt as if not even a session on the rack would straighten it out again, and his muscles had the leaden stiffness that is close cousin to cramp. But still he ran, forcing himself on, straining for the last foot-second of speed; on, on, on, when every sinew and nerve and muscle and blood vessel in his body cried for rest.

Now he was running along the road again—still keeping to the prescribed course, which was very roughly a circular tour of the district. And the pub which was his immediate goal was almost another mile along that winding road.

He heard a mechanical chugging sound behind him, and instinctively moved over to the grass verge, without slackening his pace, to let the tractor past. But then he looked, and saw that it was being driven by a girl. She had something of the summer sun in her hair, and of the mellower lights of autumn in her eyes; and not very optimistically, but because it was no time to let any straw drift by unclutched, he stuck out his thumb and made the directional gesture which is instantly understood anywhere in the world.

And the tractor stopped.

"There's a pub," he panted, climbing thankfully aboard, "less than a mile along the road. How fast do you think you could get me there?"

She rose to the challenge and got him there in just under two minutes. Which gave him plenty of time to explain that fitness was a fine ideal, but working for it could generate a thirst which was more urgent—and barely enough time to coax her address out of her on the promise that he hoped one day to thank her properly.

He dropped the heavy rucksack in the pub forecourt and waved to her as the tractor chugged off. Then he made his way in by the back door, making enough noise about it to be sure of attracting Ruth out of the obviously busy bar.

She came through at once.

"The debonair Simon Gascott," she observed, eyeing the sweat-soaked apparition; and with that minor departure from solemnity, just for once she cut a cheerier figure than the Saint himself.

"I'm in one hell of a rush," he told her gently but rapidly. "If Cawber catches us here our covers'll be royally blown. Like your friend Bert's."

In as few words as possible he told her that he would be shooting Nobbins in about four hours' time, and told her the plan that he wanted relayed to Pelton.

She listened without any outward sign of alarm or surprise.

"It had to happen," she said calmly when he had finished. "I knew his cover couldn't last. It was shaky right from the beginning."

The Saint nodded grimly. There were several things he might have said about Bert Nobbins's involvement with The Squad, but this wasn't the time or the place to say them.

He had been with Ruth only a very few minutes, and the clock that was running automatically in his head told him that the others must be getting close by now. He was already on his way through the back door when he heard the sound of a man running.

As he ducked back inside, the footsteps slowed down and stopped.

"Gascott!" he heard Cawber's voice bellow. "Where in hell are you, Gascott?"

CHAPTER 10

Cawber must have run on ahead of the others, probably to make sure that the Saint wasn't taking any shortcuts. And he must have seen the rucksack outside the pub.

So he knew that the Saint had stopped there.

And he knew that the Saint should be somewhere around.

Of course, there was a simple and obvious line that the Saint could take—that he'd got so bored with running out ahead on his own that he decided to refresh himself in this oasis, which had suddenly popped providentially into view, while he waited for all the sluggardly rest of them to catch up with him. But somehow he didn't think Cawber would buy that one.

At the very least, a suspicious mind would have something to start working on. And Cawber might even be bright enough to have a word with the customers who were just then in the bar, and discover that his track-suited quarry hadn't been in there at all. . . .

These thoughts flashed through Simon Templar's mind in no more time than it took for the echoes of Cawber's aggressively querulous shout to die away, and it was only another instant before the one possible alternative solution occurred to him—the one other possible way out, in the most literal sense.

He gripped the girl's arm urgently.

"Ruth—I noticed a gents' lavatory sign on an outside door. Now, is there a way I can get into it from here?"

"Of course," she said. "There's just the one gents' loo for the place—the outside door is locked at night. You won't need to go through the bar, either. I'll show you."

It took him a mere twenty seconds from Ruth's last words to the time when he emerged at the side of the building, to be where he had been sighted by Cawber, who was just coming out of the entrance to the public bar, beside which Simon had parked his rucksack.

That the Saint was still performing an action of the kind euphemistically known as "adjusting the dress" was a corroborative refinement which must have helped to make his alibi look convincing enough to Cawber.

Especially as Simon said blandly: "What the hell are you squawking about? Where did you think I was—up a tree?"

Cawber glared at him.

"You ain't supposed to take the pack off till you get back." Then with a note of grudging approval he added: "But I guess you're runnin' good enough. I ain't got no real complaint. Even if I don't like you, personal."

The Saint sighed.

"Cawber," he said pleasantly, as he heaved the weighty rucksack up onto his back, "if you *did* like me, personal, *then* I'd be worried."

And he jogged off down the road just as the first of the other runners came plodding into sight.

Thereafter he exerted himself only enough to finish a comfortable first, to have a waiting Lembick tick off his name on the list of runners.

"Get showered and into your civvies," Lembick ordered, with venomous restraint. "You've still got a job to do. And God help you if you muff it."

A job of a different kind.

When he shot Albert Nobbins that afternoon with so professional a detachment, the bullets were real. And Nobbins's death looked horribly convincing, right down to the blood that seeped slowly through his coat in a widening stain as he lay face down by that lake.

All the Saint could do for Nobbins was to aim the shots as far from the most certainly lethal target points as he dared—and pray that no thousand-to-one combination of improbable circumstances had intervened to stop Pelton contacting the victim in time.

Because if they had, Albert Nobbins might be a goner for real.

Rockham, at any rate, was pleased with the effect when he viewed the film that evening. The screen had been set up in his office and the curtains drawn, and Lembick and Cawber and the Saint were with him.

"You were a shade too far off when you fired," he observed ruminatively after sitting through the entertainment for the second time. "But all the same, a very creditable performance. A good clean hit."

The Saint said: "Then I've passed the final test, have I?"

"With flying colours. And I've decided to assign a leading role to you in a major job we'll be doing on Friday—the day after tomorrow. . . . What's your trouble, Lembick?" Rockham inquired silkily, as the Scot's features twisted themselves into a resentful scowl.

Lembick was bursting with it.

"It's just that Cawber and me—we've been talking, and we both feel the same about this—" He seemed to have difficulty stifling a pejorative strong enough to convey their dislike and distrust: "—this new man."

"This new man who thrashed you in your own gym—yes, Lembick, what about him?"

"It's not that—not the fight." Lembick twisted his big hands together as if he wished he had them around the Saint's neck. "But he's—it's his *attitude*." Again he scowled and seemed to be groping for a word extreme enough to express his condemnation. "He's too goddam *flip!*"

"He's a good man," said Rockham, suddenly hard and inflexible.

"Better than us?" demanded Lembick.

"A different type," Rockham said flatly.

"We've been with you from the start," Cawber said sulkily.

"And you'll stay to the end."

Lembick said: "We just don't want him promoted over our heads."

Rockham eyed them coldly.

"This is a military formation," he snapped, "not a labour union." Anger blazed for a moment in those near-transparent eyes. "Now get out, both of you. And take the cine gear."

When the two trainers had gone, Rockham poured port for himself and Simon from the crystal decanter in the corner cabinet.

He brought the drinks and said: "You have a taste for the good life, Gascott."

"Who hasn't?"

Rockham shrugged.

"Lembick, Cawber. They only work for the money. And the chance it gives them to boss and bully a number of subordinates that I supply."

The Saint saw the likely drift of Rockham's thought, and decided that his best course was to play up to him.

"Natural-born deputy Führers," he said, nodding.

"Ah! You agree!"

The Saint raised an eyebrow that asked if disagreement were sanely possible.

"That the world's divided?" he rasped. "Shepherds and sheep? Of course. It always has been and it always will be."

Rockham beamed.

"You understand! But so few people do. And yet it's so simple. Some men are born to lead, others to follow."

"That's for sure," the Saint said, drawing him out.

"It's always been the one sure thing. Once you've grasped that —once you've freed your thinking from all this democratic garbage —*then* you can act."

"As long as you're one of the lucky tribe of born leaders."

"Luckily for us, we both are." Rockham drank with evident enjoyment, studying the Saint for a while before he spoke again. He said: "It's three years now since I made the break with society— with the law. But most of all with the unworkable idea that men are equal—in anything. Democracy!" He thumped a fist on the table. "Democracy is dedicated to the protection of the weak and the stupid."

"Numbers against quality," rasped the Saint sycophantically.

Rockham put down the glass and stroked his square jaw with that hand whose potent karate chop Simon had seen in action.

"We speak the same language, you and I. I sensed it from the start. Most men—you said it yourself—are no better than sheep.

They're fit for nothing but to be herded about. Mindless obedient imbeciles! Or they're like chess pieces—expendable, all but the king, in the larger interest of the game. Most men are only fit to be shuffled about like pawns—forces to be marshalled, pitted against one another . . . sacrificed."

" 'And one by one, back in the closet lays,' " the Saint quoted.

"Exactly," the other man agreed, evidently recognising the line. "But what the verse doesn't say is that when Destiny moves men about on the chessboard of life, it operates through other men. Through the leaders, Gascott. Through men like you and me."

While he was talking, he had strolled over to a small square table that stood between two armchairs near the drinks cabinet.

"I believe you're a chess player yourself," he said; and he slid most of the tabletop aside to expose an inlaid board with a hollowed-out compartment at either end holding the pieces.

"I've occasionally done a bit of wood-pushing," Simon admitted, as Rockham picked out a white and a black pawn.

Rockham said: "I'm interested to see what kind of a game you play." And there was an odd, almost fanatical glint in his eye as he spoke.

He shuffled the two pawns about behind his back, according to the established schoolboyish convention of the game, and then brought his closed hands into view to offer Simon the choice.

He chose. Rockham opened the hand and showed the black pawn.

"I have the advantage of the move, I think," he said after they had rapidly set out the pieces and sat down. And he pushed a white pawn two squares forward along one of the centre files.

The Saint made an exactly matching move, which left the two pawns head on to each other in the middle of the board.

"Pawn to king four, pawn to king four," Rockham commented as he brought out his king's knight on its devious lopsided course. "Let's see what you do with knight to KB3."

Again the Saint made the same move, leaving the position symmetrical; and then Rockham slid a bishop forward through the gap that his advancing pawn had left, and once more Simon made an exactly complementary move from his own side of the board.

Rockham eyed him shrewdly.

"Hmm. You join me in *Giuoco Piano*. Probably the way most games at amateur level begin—but also the classic of classic openings. The quiet game."

"Mentioned in the Göttingen manuscript of fourteen ninety," the Saint concurred.

"You do know your chess," Rockham smiled. "But let's see if we can't do something to hot things up." And the smile faded as he advanced another of his white pawns two squares, on a file nearer the queen's side of the board, so that it threatened to capture, on the next move, the bishop Simon had advanced.

But there was nothing to prevent the bishop from taking the pawn in a pre-emptive strike right there and then.

The Saint sat back and eyed the board for a moment.

Then he commented encyclopaedically: "Evans Gambit. An interesting line. The aim is to prevent black's pawn to queen four and to attack the weak spot at his KB2. White offers a free pawn, and in return he gets—possibly—a winning attack. This particular gambit was thought up a hundred and twenty years ago—appropriately enough by a soldier, Captain W. D. Evans. And it's been used by a host of world-class players since. Bird, Blackman, Staunton, Anderssen—"

"Morphy, Steinity—" Rockham continued the list with enthusiasm. "But it's the conception, man—the strategic *conception* of a gambit, any gambit—that's so magnificent. Don't you agree? To sacrifice a minor piece, early in the game, so as to give yourself time to manoeuvre, space to attack. The idea couldn't be bolder or simpler. You put yourself at limited risk, to open up the battlefield or to make a quick strike. And then—" He made a rapid throat-cutting movement with his hand. "Of course, it's a gamble. If you can't capitalise on the sacrifice, if your attack collapses, all your forces are in danger. But if you can, if you can! Then what a magnificent strategic beginning the pawn gambit is!"

The Saint inclined his head, acknowledging the point but with reservation.

"Still," he said, "gambits can be refuted, and often are. This one included. And the best way to refute a gambit is to accept it." With one swift pass of his hand the presumptuous white pawn was gone and the black bishop was in its place. "Do your worst."

He dropped the pawn into one of the recesses in the table; Rockham blinked at the prestidigitatory feat, and then moved up another pawn to threaten the black bishop again.

"The second pawn," he said, eyeing the Saint keenly, "is properly protected. Now you're going to have to withdraw that episcopal venturer in one direction or another, I'm afraid."

"True enough," admitted the Saint, imperturbably making just such a strategic retreat.

They played on for a while, without any serious edge of competition to the game; until Rockham suggested they abandon it as a draw.

"The position's more or less equal," he said. "I can see you're a worthy opponent. Sometime we'll have a marathon. Soon. But there's something I want to show you, now."

The Saint watched as he crossed to the wall safe and twiddled the combination dial. He brought out a small leather bag and spilled the contents out on the table.

The contents consisted of a large handful of irregularly shaped glassy beads with a semi-opaque sheen to them.

"Uncut diamonds," Rockham said. "One hundred thousand pounds in negotiable, transportable pebbles!" And Simon Templar knew at a glance that those pebbles were exactly what Rockham said they were, and were worth every penny of the figure he had named.

"Nice," said the Saint, and meant it.

"A down payment on Friday's job," Rockham crowed. "It's a form of currency I much prefer to large cheques." He picked up a half-handful of the diamonds and let them trickle in a miniature waterfall into the other hand. "Beautiful, aren't they? Concentrated wealth."

"Friday's job must be a big one," Simon observed casually, "if that little lot's just the down payment."

Rockham eyed him speculatively.

"You'll be briefed in the morning," he said. "But you'll have a starring role, all right. And I can tell you one thing: the prize you'll be after, the prize that my—clients put such a high value on, is a man!"

Rockham gathered up the diamonds carefully and poured them

back into the little leather bag. His eyes had never left them for one instant the whole time they had been on the table.

Simon Templar too had his moments of concentrated attention from which it would have been difficult to deflect him. For example, he watched now with expert interest as Rockham locked the little bag of diamonds away in the safe; and he had watched with even greater interest a little earlier, when that same safe was being opened.

CHAPTER 11

When he kept a prearranged rendezvous at Ruth's car that night, outside the wall, she drove him just a few miles towards Petersfield for a conference with Pelton—and an Albert Nobbins who was somewhat the worse for wear.

"I'm glad you managed to keep all the bullets in the area of the bullet-proofing," Nobbins told him.

"I'm only sorry you had to go through the experience at all," Simon sympathised, looking hard at Pelton. "A Wilkinson vest is a lot better than nothing, but you must be feeling pretty sore all the same."

"Badly bruised, all right." Nobbins put a brave face on it, but he looked pale and shaken.

"At least, I hope there are no bones broken." To Pelton the Saint said: "But why the conference?"

Colonel Pelton put his neat fingertips together and tilted his head over, pigeonlike.

"The answer's in a name," he said. "James Anthony Instrood. Head of the European Desk, Chinese espionage. In other words, the man in charge of their whole network in Western Europe. The man the Resident Directors take their orders from."

The Saint raised a lazy eyebrow and looked politely impressed.

"What about him?"

"Normally he stays in Peking. But a couple of days ago he slipped over to Hong Kong—there's a girl, it seems. And we managed to grab him. We've been waiting for this chance for years."

"Sounds like quite a prize," Simon agreed. "What are you doing with him?"

"Bringing him to the U.K. for interrogation." Pelton smiled faintly. "Which Mr Nobbins here will begin."

Nobbins went a little pinker.

"He's got more useful information in his little finger than a whole sackful of Chinese agents," he said. "Of course, he'll take time to break. But when he does . . ."

"When he does, we could knock out half the Chinese network," Pelton said drily. "*If* he does. So you can see how important he is to us—and to the Chinese."

"They'll want him back pretty badly. . . ." The Saint tugged reflectively at his moustache. The connection was obvious enough, but the words had to be said, so he said them. "You're working on the assumption that the Chinese may be Rockham's current employers—bearing in mind his recent visitors?"

"I believe that to be a hypothesis to which we should give consideration," Pelton said pedantically.

Simon Templar gave consideration to the hypothesis for a moment.

"Rockham's certainly hatching something big," he said, feeling under no obligation at that moment to mention the down payment he had seen. "And it's a man-snatch, all right—of some kind. But that's about all I know. Except that I'm going to be in on it myself, and I'm due for a briefing in the morning, and the job's scheduled for the next day—Friday."

Pelton's eyes narrowed thoughtfully.

"That would fit the hypothesis very well," he said. "Instrood's plane arrives late tomorrow night. "We're landing him at Blackbushe and he'll be driven under convoy guard straight to Braizedown Hall, which is just a few miles away. The debriefing will begin at once. Any operation to abduct him would need to be mounted very fast."

"Instrood won't be worth a red cent to the Chinks once he's spilled the beans," Nobbins put in superfluously.

"And Friday," Pelton continued, undeflected by his subordinate's contribution, "is about as soon as Rockham could sensibly plan to make some kind of rescue bid. I'm assuming that if he *is* aiming to snatch Instrood back for the Chinese, then he has access to inside information, as usual. Which means he knows when and how we're bringing Instrood into the country, and he may even know where we're taking him."

"All this is more or less speculative for the present," Simon pointed out. "But if your analysis is correct, what's to stop you changing the venue for putting the matches under Comrade Instrood's toes, preferably at the last minute?"

David Pelton's glittering dark eyes darted over the faces of the other three.

"We've given it careful thought." He looked at Nobbins, who nodded. "And our conclusion is that if Rockham *has* got this commission from the Chinese, then the time has come when we can't afford to leave his activities unchecked any longer. The Squad will have to be wiped out. If that's the league they've got into, they're too dangerous to be left alone any longer."

"I see," said the Saint slowly; and he meant more by that than either Pelton or Nobbins or Ruth Barnaby realised. "So if Rockham's a big enough fish to be dangerous, he'll swim straight into the net. Or you hope he will."

"Exactly." Pelton smiled faintly again, the merest quiver of the lips. "If Rockham makes a bid to get James Anthony Instrood away from us, he's going to run into much more than he bargained for. His forces will be divided—one party on the raid, and the rest back at base. And we'll have the advantage of surprise—as well as a man in the enemy camp."

"You mean in the firing line," said the Saint.

Pelton shrugged.

"If you're in charge of the raiding party, so much the better—so long as you remember to dodge the bullets when the crucial moment comes. But we'll be relying on your help beforehand—we'll need to know what sort of attack he intends to mount, so that we can prepare to meet it at minimum risk to our own forces."

"The probabilities look right," Simon said as he stood up. "But it's still guesswork at this stage. I'll pass on whatever I find out tomorrow." He paused, looking speculatively at Pelton. "By the way, just so that I can settle a bet with myself—are you a chess player, by any chance?"

Pelton looked mildly surprised and said: "As a matter of fact, yes. I enjoy a game occasionally. Why do you ask?"

"Just tell me what your favourite opening is," Simon said, "the one you like to use yourself, when you're playing as White, let's say."

"King's Gambit," Pelton said. "Or one of the other pawn gambits."

"Thanks," said the Saint with the ghost of a smile. "I just won a bet with myself."

On the short drive back, Ruth asked him about that parting remark.

"I don't know the game," she said. "What did you mean—about openings, and gambits?"

"It would take too long to explain now," he told her. "Let's just say I discovered something your boss has in common with Rockham."

His occasional excursions to the wall and over had become almost routine by now, and in a few minutes he was back in his room, his denims, shirt, and pullover were neatly folded over the chair, and the black plimsolls neatly aligned under it, with absolutely no sign of any hurry in the manner of their arrangement. And in a few minutes more he really was peacefully asleep again, as if he had done nothing else since going to bed the night before.

In those few minutes, however, he had administered himself a sober warning: not to push his luck with these nocturnal excursions too far. Until then, Lembick and Cawber had had no reason to be suspicious of him and hence to subject him to special surveillance. Now, even without suspicion, they had motives to look for or even to manufacture some evidence that would discredit him. And it could hardly be long before even their slower wits visualised his room as a tempting site for some nefarious operation.

He was roused in the morning by a weird sound that droned mystifyingly over the blurred threshold of his consciousness. At first it seemed like the despairing death-cry of a stricken poltergeist . . . or was it a wailing banshee come to mourn in anticipation of an imminent human demise . . . or was there some still more unearthly explanation that would occur to him once he was properly awake? It was a plaintive penetrating sound that rose and fell in ear-torturing cadences, a plangent ululation such as never came from the mouth of man nor beast.

The Saint rolled out of bed and looked out of the window.

It was Lembick, playing the bagpipes.

Nor was this torture inflicted on his fellows for his own private pleasure, a fact that became clear when Rockham briefed him that morning for the next day's mission.

Rockham gave away no more than he had to. What he did give away included the name Instrood, and the location: Braizedown Hall.

"It's a straightforward enough plan," he said. "I'm briefing you separately as you'll be playing the part of Officer in Command.

"But don't run away with the idea that you're in command of the mission," he added. "Because I'll be there myself, right beside you. As your Corporal."

"That's nice and trusting of you," said the Saint.

Rockham turned those pale eyes on him.

"A good mercenary commander never separates himself for long from his troops," he replied. "Now—Braizedown Hall is under constant guard. A platoon of men, day and night. We could always try storming the place with superior numbers, but there's a neater way. We take the place of the guard."

Simon raised an eyebrow.

"How?"

"The Paras are due to hand over tomorrow to another regiment. The Lowland Light Infantry. And we've enough of their uniforms to make up a plausible-looking platoon. Lembick has an encyclopaedic knowledge of the Scots regiments. I've put him in charge of the drill."

The Saint thought about it. It was a bold and yet simple idea, the sort he would have expected from Rockham. He looked appraisingly at this man with the big square head, the determined jaw, the powerful hands; and he wondered what sort of conventional military strategist he would have made, if he had not chosen the path of lawless violence.

"What about the real platoon?" he asked.

"We divert them—send them on a circular tour around the country," said Rockham, smiling. "And then we roll up in their place. And within twenty minutes after that, we roll out again—with the valuable Mr Instrood."

All that day, the selected group of twenty-five men were drilled by Lembick in their tartan trews and battle-blouses. Tam-o'-Shanters, those peculiarly Scottish woolen berets worn aslant, completed the uniform of that unique regiment—a regiment so elite and exclusive that even a person knowledgeable in military affairs of the time might be forgiven for never having heard of the Lowland Light Infantry.

Simon himself received special detailed briefing from Lembick on his role as Captain—and more than once he drew thankfully on his hasty studies to supply the general knowledge that was assumed of him.

When he woke himself that night for his rendezvous with Ruth Barnaby, it was with a simultaneous reprise of the cautionary thought with which he had fallen asleep after his last sortie. He made his way to the toilet as usual, but before switching on the light he took a long look out of the window. And in the darkness below, he detected at one point the intermittent red glow of a cigarette, like an overstimulated glowworm.

Therefore, after making normal use of the plumbing, instead of returning to his room or using the drainpipe exit route that he had established, he went boldly down the stairs and ambled out of the bedroom block.

He stood briefly outside the door, breathing in the cool night air and now and again gazing up at the few faint stars that were visible. When his eyes had adjusted fully to the dark, he began a leisurely stroll around. As soon as he moved off he saw out of the corner of his eye the black shadow that detached itself from a wall of the next block; and throughout the unhurried circuit he made of the main buildings he knew that the shadow was following at a discreet distance behind him.

The Saint smiled indulgently and allowed the pantomime to continue until he chose the moment to make an abrupt about-turn and say: "Why not join me, chum, instead of trailing along like a lost beagle?"

It was Lembick who loomed recognisably out of the dark. And said: "Where d'ye think you're going?"

"For a walk," said the Saint imperturbably. "I got fidgets—tossing and turning, couldn't sleep."

"Nerves, maybe?" Lembick sneered. "About the job tomorrow?"

"No nerves," rasped the Saint, in the abrasive tones of Gascott. "It's a sort of muscle restlessness. Stops you settling down to sleep. The only cure is to move around and work it off."

"You must need more exercise," Lembick said. "That can be arranged."

The Saint stood and faced him.

"Lembick," he said, with a kind of military authority that he knew would have effect, "let's stop this nonsense. We're in this together now. We've got to work together. Let's call it quits and get on with it." He stuck out his hand disarmingly. "Okay?"

After a long pause, Lembick accepted the hand.

"Okay," he growled. "For now."

"Then I'll go jog off my fidgets," Simon said amicably.

"Okay," Lembick said. "Just don't get mixed up with the patrol."

"And you stay out of my room," Simon responded genially. "In case you get any ideas, I'll warn you: the feelthy pictures in my bag are booby-trapped."

He strolled away on his supposed therapeutic walk through the grounds with the intuitive certainty that his bull-by-the-horns ploy had neutralised Lembick for that night at least. But he was under no illusion that he could count on it to work indefinitely.

That was a problem which would have to be dealt with in what cliché-mongers conveniently dispose of as "due course." Until then, there was no worthwhile guarantee whatever of what form that nebulous futurity would actually take.

CHAPTER 12

Ruth Barnaby was waiting for him outside the wall as arranged, and he told her about the briefing and drills.

"So it's on," he concluded. "Pelton's hypothesis was right. Target—Instrood. At Worplesford Cross, all being well, the genuine platoon go off on a wild-goose chase, and we roll up at Braizedown in their place. The guard change is scheduled for five o'clock, and we'll be at Worplesford before four-thirty."

"I'll tell Pelton," she said.

"Will the Lowlanders be put in the picture?"

"I don't know. That'll be Pelton's decision. I'd guess not. It just might get back to Rockham."

The Saint sighed as he uncoiled himself from the car seat beside her.

"Ruth—I'm sure you're right. That's probably exactly what your boss will say." Simon had got out of the car, and now he paused on his way, leaning in through the open door. "But if Pelton won't confide in the Lowlanders, I hope he'll damn well confide in *somebody*. Because otherwise," he said with heavy emphasis, "who the hell's going to form that powerful reception party he promised?"

And she was still pondering the implications of those words for some time after she watched him ease his long figure back up to the rope ladder and over the wall.

So the curtain was about to go up, he mused, on what looked like being the final act in one of the strangest dramas he had ever been mixed up in. But while he slept that night, another scene of the penultimate act was being played out in another rural setting, not twenty miles away.

From an upstairs window of Braizedown Hall, Ruth Barnaby

and Albert Nobbins watched as three vehicles came to a halt in the crunching gravel outside the front door.

First a jeep, decorated with the blue-on-maroon winged horse of the Parachute Regiment; in the driving-seat a Corporal of the Regiment and beside him a Captain. Then the big dark-green official car normally used by Pelton. Then a three-ton army lorry bearing the same insignia as the jeep.

"You think you can break him?" Ruth Barnaby asked.

Nobbins shrugged. He had changed his usual spectacles for a pair with round steel-rimmed lenses that made him look harder, less sympathetic.

"He's a trained agent," he said. "And tougher than most, so they say. But we're calling the tune. And I've got him for a week. All to myself."

Nobbins's mouth came down in a firm little line and his manner held tense purposefulness that she had never seen in him before.

They watched as two paratroopers armed with Sten guns jumped down off the back of the truck. Four men got out of the car—the driver, two regimental policemen in red berets and white webbing and wearing the black-on-red RP armbands, and a man in a straitjacket and a black hood that completely covered his head.

"James Anthony Instrood," said Nobbins softly.

"I'll leave you to it, then," she said.

"Remember," he called to her as she went out, "no word about The Squad to Captain Yates or any of the Paras at this stage."

Nobbins sat back behind the desk. There were two lamps on it, angled to point about three feet above the seat of the empty chair facing him. For the tenth time he switched the lamps on and slightly adjusted the position of the powerful beams, then switched them off again.

There was a knock at the door.

Captain Yates and his Corporal pushed Instrood forward into the room.

"Delivery of the prisoner, sir."

"Thank you, Captain. I take it Colonel Pelton checked him at Blackbushe?"

"Yes, sir."

"Then that'll be all, Captain. But you'll leave the Corporal on the door, of course."

"Sir." They withdrew and shut the door.

Nobbins undid some straps of the straitjacket; then he loosened the drawstring around Instrood's neck and lifted off the hood.

"Sit down, Instrood. Cigarette?" He gestured at a box on the desk.

Instrood shook his head, smiling scornfully.

"I'm familiar with interrogation technique. A bit of kindness— then the rough stuff." He shrugged. "Sometimes it works."

"But not with James Anthony Instrood?"

"Not with me."

The two men looked remarkably alike. Nobbins saw that Instrood too was a small man, bulging somewhat at the waist, and that he too wore glasses with steel-rimmed circular lenses. He was rather older than Nobbins, his colouring rather darker, and the three-day stubble on his face gave a tougher line to his jaw; but the two of them were similar enough in general appearance to have been brothers.

Instrood smiled again, with a contemptuous curl to his lips, and said: "You don't really expect to get anywhere with this, do you, Nobbins?"

"You'll crack inside a week, Instrood," Nobbins said, with more conviction than he felt.

Instrood smiled that thin withering smile again, and said nothing.

"You'll talk!" Nobbins said, provoked. "Before we're done you'll *beg* me to listen!"

Viciously he snapped on the two spotlights. Instrood sighed patiently, sank a little lower in his chair, and closed his eyes.

"Ask your questions, then," he said resignedly.

"You know what I want from you."

"Names of Resident Directors, cutouts, agents—the communication chain? Yes, of course I know," Instrood said wearily.

"On September the nineteenth two agents were dispatched to Paris—a French couple," Nobbins intoned. "Who were they?"

"Abelard and Heloise."

Nobbins leaned forward eagerly.

"Their code names?"

He realised he had made a fool of himself the moment the words were out of his mouth. Instrood sniggered. Nobbins boiled with fury.

"Communications network?" he demanded, on a shriller note. "Your Resident Director for Germany? For Italy? For Holland?"

Instrood shook his head.

"Nothing doing."

"Names, details, facts!" Nobbins almost screamed the words as he thumped the desk. "I want facts!"

He switched off the two spotlights abruptly and sank back in his chair. Instrood opened his eyes and saw the beads of sweat standing out on the simmering Nobbins's brow. He smiled to himself.

"I'll give you some facts," he said in a quietly reasonable, almost friendly tone. "Listen. Ten years ago I did your job. A bit higher up the ladder maybe, but the same sort of job. I lived on eight hundred a year and haggled for every two quids' worth of expenses."

"And then you threw it all over for Peking—I know."

"Where I've lived like a lord. Anything I wanted—cars, girls, the best food and wine—the good life."

"And these were the facts you were going to give me?" Nobbins said scornfully. "All you've told me is that you've been living high on the hog. So what?"

"So I don't forget it. Ten years ago I chose. And that's the kind of choice you only make once. I've chosen—I'm not going back on it."

Nobbins studied Instrood and was conscious again of the similarities between them. Yet there was difference, too—the important difference between self-confidence and uncertainty, success and failure, a difference that could somehow give the prisoner a moral advantage over his jailer.

"You're finished, Instrood," he said, as if reciting a formula. "Those days are over for you now. Why not make it easy for yourself?"

"You mean easy for you. But why should I? Time's on my side."

"No cooperation, then?" Nobbins said mechanically.

"Voluntary? No."

"But you'll crack, sooner or later."

"Every man does, when the real treatment begins." Instrood shrugged. "Oh yes, I'll crack—in the end."

"But not till it's too late?"

"Exactly. Not till agents have been replaced, lines of communication changed. . . . I'll crack, all right. But not yet. And you won't be the man to do it."

"How can you be so sure?"

"You're a loser," Instrood said more gently. "I can tell. Remember, I was like you, once. I was a loser. Time was, I wouldn't have said boo to a goose. And they, these people"—he looked with distaste around the shabby office—"they never valued me, never appreciated me for what I was worth. But the Chinese did. They gave me power, gave me room to develop! The Chinese made me what I am today!"

And there was something very strong and sure and tough about Instrood as he leaned forward and flicked the switches of the two lamps on the desk so that his own face was flooded again with their dazzling light.

"Now I expect you'll be anxious to get on to the nasty stuff— Mr Nobbins," he said; and he settled back into the chair, with contempt registering in his features as plainly as before.

CHAPTER 13

"All right, carry on, Corporal." The Saint barked out the order with military crispness.

"Sir," said Rockham, saluting smartly. Then to the men: "Squad—fall in!"

It was Friday morning—the last rehearsal for their afternoon mission.

"All right, lads." Rockham was once again the calm commanding officer, his Corporal's uniform notwithstanding. "This is the final check. For today's fun and games you've got to look as Scottish as haggis."

His gaze roamed over the line of men, their tartan trews and their tunics immaculately pressed, their rifles held parallel, their boots identically gleaming, their Tam-o'-Shanters identically angled.

To Lembick he said: "Satisfied with all the details?"

"The Lowland Lights themselves would be proud of them, sir."

"There'll be no room for mistakes, Lembick."

"You can rely on me."

They arrived at Worplesford Cross three-quarters of an hour later, Rockham and the Saint travelling in the jeep and the others in the three-tonner which had also been decorated with a small square of the Regiment's distinctive tartan on the front fender. It took the Saint and Rockham another half hour to erect the diversion signs reading

WORPLESFORD VILLAGE AND BRAIZEDOWN
—TEMPORARY ROUTE

at four strategically chosen junctions, ending up with the last sign at Worplesford Cross itself.

"That'll give 'em a pleasant little round tour," Rockham said with satisfaction.

The men and vehicles were well hidden under cover of a sparse wood near the junction when presently the real McCoy roared into view. The fake Lowlanders watched the jeep and lorry—bearing that same tartan patch—slow down at the sign, hesitate, then turn off exactly as they were supposed to do.

Rockham started the jeep, and the Saint heard the lorry's engine clatter into life behind them.

And then they saw Ruth Barnaby's car.

Ruth was driving. Beside her sat Lembick, with his revolver trained on her.

Lembick gestured with the gun, and she stopped and got out. He grabbed her by one arm and marched her to the jeep. "Look what I found. In the trees further along."

"The young lady who works at the Bull, isn't it?" Rockham stroked his chin impassively.

The Saint's pulses and his thoughts were racing, but outwardly he wore the sort of expression Rockham might have expected Gascott to be wearing—interested, concerned, but not personally involved.

"The little bitch had us under observation," Lembick said.

"Did she, now?" said Rockham thoughtfully.

"And she was in contact with somebody, on a small portable radio."

"That's worse." Simon could almost hear the motors humming efficiently in Rockham's brain as he weighed the possibilities dispassionately. "Did you catch her before the real Lowlanders went off at a tangent, or after?"

"Just before."

"So she won't have reported the switch to whoever it was." He turned his cold clear eyes on her. "I wonder if we've time to persuade her to—confide in us." She returned his stare with a defiant toss of the head. "No, perhaps not . . . But we'll need to decide quickly whether to proceed with the job. What do you think, Gascott?"

"I say go on," Simon rasped. "I'd lay ten to one she's working for your client." He barely gave the girl a glance. "Inspecting his contractors on the job!"

Lembick stabbed a sudden accusing forefinger at him.

"Cawber saw *him* at the pub!" he snapped triumphantly. "During the cross-country race. He stopped to go to the loo. Or so *we*'re meant to think! But I know what *I* think. I think he's in with *her*. This whole thing stinks of a set-up! I say abort!"

"I'm getting pretty tired of these accusations," the Saint said, bristling. "Let's get on with the job."

Rockham switched his calm level glance back and forth between them.

"Difficult," he said after a pause. "But on balance—we go on." Suddenly he was totally decisive. "Put her in the back of the truck, Lembick. And tell Cawber to stay with her in the truck at the other end and keep her out of sight. I daresay we can manage with one man less in the platoon—and I never did find him a very convincing Scot. Now let's get rolling."

With a last murderous glance at the Saint, Lembick dragged her off.

Rockham spoke only once during the two-mile drive to Braizedown Hall.

He said blandly: "Exercise, I believe, is usually dehydrating. Or do you have a weak bladder? Anyhow, why didn't you just stop behind any tree?"

"It wasn't my bladder, it was my bowels," Simon said bluntly, seeing no better answer, and conscious of Rockham's pistol holster against his hip. "Something I must have had to eat at your health farm. But I guess Lembick will never be happy till he can hang something on me."

Rockham's silence seemed to accept the explanation, at least for the moment, but the Saint had an uncomfortable feeling that his act had taken a funambulist turn and that the rope was wearing perilously thin.

There were two sentries on the gate at Braizedown, paratroopers wearing the RP armband. They saluted and let the jeep and truck through to park in front of the guard hut, behind the similar vehicles of the outgoing Paras platoon. The main body of the Paras themselves were standing in loose formation along one side of the drive.

Captain Yates came across to the jeep as Rockham and the Saint got out.

Simon saluted smartly, and Yates returned the salute of his equal in rank.

"C Platoon, B Company, Second Battalion Lowland Light Infantry," Simon said briskly. "One officer, twenty-eight men, reporting for guard duty."

"Trust the Lowland Lights to be regimental about it," Yates smiled. "We're inclined to take things a bit more casually, I'm afraid." He handed the Saint a millboard. "Send a couple of men to relieve the guard on the prisoner, sign here, and he's all yours."

The uniformed mercenaries of The Squad had already poured from the back of the truck and assembled loosely, facing the Paras across the drive. The Saint called to two of them.

"Ewan, McCann—up to the house. Relieve the guard on the prisoner. Take the jeep."

Simon searched Yates's features, and thought he saw a flicker of uneasiness pass across that phlegmatic face. He wondered how much he knew.

As the Saint figured it, Ruth would have been in contact by radio either with Yates himself or, perhaps, with Pelton. But either way, she had been interrupted before the switch—so no one could be certain that a switch *had been* yet. Unless the Paras had got together with the real Lowlanders earlier, so that they'd recognise them when the time came. But somehow he didn't see that as very likely, knowing Pelton's established preference for confiding as little as possible to as few people as possible. How much had he told Yates—if anything?

As the two men he had detailed to relieve the guard on Instrood jumped into the jeep and drove off up the short driveway, the Saint turned to Rockham.

"All right, Corporal. Fall in the men."

The two squads came to attention under the orders of their respective NCO's.

"Piper!" called the Saint, hiding his profound unenthusiasm for this act in the proceedings; and Lembick obediently appeared with the bagpipes.

Simon made his inspection of the outgoing guard as cursory as he could, while the pipes skirled out behind him in an ear-torturing dirge.

Yates crossed to inspect the new guard. He eyed the first man. Then his gaze swept along the rank, and back.

The men were lined up just as in their drills—trews and tunics immaculate, boots gleaming, rifles in perfect alignment, Tam-o'-Shanters neatly aslant over the left ear.

Yates looked again at the man in front of him—at his hat. And then, with a furrow of puzzlement creasing his brow, he half-turned his head to look questioningly at the Saint.

At his headgear.

"The Tammies!" Yates shouted suddenly. "Lowland Lights slant 'em to the right!" You're phonies!"

So whether Yates had been tipped off or not, apparently Lembick, the reliable expert on Scottish military traditions, had goofed it.

And both of those were possible eventualities on which the Saint had not been tipped off. He had only his instincts and his reflexes to cue him.

Rockham had his revolver out and was swinging it around to point at Yates before the Paras Captain had finished speaking. The Saint hurled himself at Rockham just as his finger tightened on the trigger, knocking him sideways to the ground, and the bullet whistled by Yates's ear.

"Yates—I'm Templar—with you!" Simon called to him as the Squad men raised their rifles.

"Scatter, men!" Yates yelled. "Fire at will! But not at the Captain!"

Both groups of uniformed men scattered. Simon ducked behind the Paras' jeep as the shots rang out from both sides; and then fluently cursing the tardiness of Pelton's reinforcements, he worked his way around towards the back of their lorry. Between there and The Squad's own lorry was a twenty-foot gap.

He put his head down and sprinted those few yards; but someone must have been watching, because a bullet lifted the Tam-o'-

Shanter clean off his head and he felt the wind of deadly passing breath. Then he reached the lorry, and thankfully took cover on the side of it away from the shooting.

He knew Ruth was still in that truck with Cawber. Assuming Pelton's reinforcements did eventually arrive, there was no telling how Cawber would react. He might try to use the girl as a shield or hostage to save his own skin; or he might panic and shoot her. And as there was something the Saint wanted to say to her before anything too final happened to her, the first task he had set himself now was to get her away from Cawber.

His guess was that Cawber would have moved right to the back of the truck when the shooting started, and would be craning his neck, peeping round the far side of the tailboard, to watch the action.

And the Saint's guess was right, as he saw when he peered cautiously round the truck's rear end from his own safe side. Cawber was sitting so that he could watch the battle without serious risk of getting his head blown off and still keep tabs on Ruth. He had her gripped by the arm, and the fingers of his other hand were curled loosely around the trigger of a Sten gun.

He glanced aside and, for one fragmentary instant, saw the man he knew as Gascott, and saw the automatic that was levelled at his own heart.

And the Saint shot him dead, without hesitation and without remorse, before he could even move.

"Thank you," Ruth said calmly.

Simon had no time to compliment her on her sang-froid. He unhitched the tailgate of the truck and helped her down; and then he said:

"I'm making a run for the house. You'd better come along too. You know the layout."

As an afterthought, he hauled himself up into the back of the truck. Cawber's fingers had tightened on the Sten gun in his death spasm. Simon prised them open, wrenched the gun from that involuntary grip, and thrust it into the girl's hands.

"You'd better have this—just in case. I'm sure you know how to use it."

They took a roundabout route, skirting some trees, and zigzagging their way from one truck's shelter to the next. The shots were still stuttering out, with the two sides having scattered rapidly behind the available cover.

When they stopped for a short breather, she said: "You're thinking of Instrood?"

He nodded.

"Not that it's likely that anyone'll have harmed him. But that's not a chance we should take. And I saw Rockham heading this way."

They saw some fallen men, and once the Saint pointed savagely and gripped the girl's arm.

"Look at those poor bastards! A couple of Yates's men—and they look like goners. What the *hell* does Pelton think he's playing at?" he blazed.

She shrugged, as if to say that Pelton's ways were mysterious, and not for mere mortals to question; and the Saint's mouth set in a still harder line as they ran on towards the gaunt grey structure that was the house.

Further on he pointed again at two more prone figures, this time in the Lowlanders' uniform.

"The two men I detailed to relieve the guard on Instrood," he said. "I wonder what happened to the two Paras they were relieving."

They approached the house cautiously, from the rear. The Saint kicked open the back door while they stood as well clear as they could of anything that might come through it. Nothing did, and they were about to go in, when suddenly she clutched at his arm, dragging him aside a split second before the crack of a shot.

But the bullet didn't smash its way into the wall where the Saint had been; and neither did it dissipate its lethal energy by ploughing into the Saint himself.

It ended up somewhere in the depths of Lembick's skull.

They took in the scene, and understood it, in less than the blink of an eye, as a camera occasionally captures a moment of such graphically telling summary as to make comment totally superfluous.

They saw Lembick, with his gun pointing to where Simon Templar had been and with an unsightly hole in his forehead; and

they saw Rockham, his own gun levelled in his hand. Rockham
had dealt out his own ruthless punishment to Lembick for the
mistake that had spiked the mission.

That was all; and after that one single snapshot instant the
Saint and Ruth Barnaby dived into the house, and Rockham's
next bullet came spewing out of the gun to splinter harmlessly
into the wood of the door as the Saint slammed it behind them.

"My turn to thank you," he said gently; and after such a narrow
escape as that, they would have been less than human if for a few
seconds he hadn't put his arms around her and felt her cling to
him with an answering warmth, even while his eyes, and his gun,
had to stay unwaveringly on the door.

She detached herself and said: "This is a business assignment,
Simon."

And her eyes were as cool and their expression as detached as
ever.

He nodded briskly.

"You know where to look for Instrood?"

"Yes."

"All right. I'll stay here in case Rockham decides to come after
us. And, Ruth—go carefully."

"I'm a trained agent, remember?" she said, and moved off with
the Sten gun held at the ready.

The Saint hadn't the smallest doubt that Rockham would come
after them. When she had gone he backed away from the door, in
the same direction, and stationed himself in the big hallway, near
the foot of the stairs, where he could watch for an approach from
either front or back.

What he was not expecting was an approach from above.

Rockham must have climbed up a fire escape and gone in by an
upstairs window, then crept to the staircase. He was halfway down
before Simon whirled at the faint sound. But it was too late—
Rockham already had the drop on him, and the hollow snout of
Rockham's gun could be seen from the receiving end to be
pointed accurately enough to score on any standing target.

Therefore the only escape would be if, at the instant of explo-
sion, the target was not standing where it had been.

If there had been time to think about it all, the Saint might well have had to conclude that the moment he had cheated so many times in his career of devil-may-care outlawry had come at last to claim him. But then, if he had had time to think, he would have taken too long to act, however hopelessly.

He had time for neither. He had only the eye-searing moment, the microcosmic instant of realisation, as he watched John Rockham's knuckle whitening on the trigger.

In the only possible ultimate instant, he flung himself aside.

The crash of the shot was deafening, but he felt no impact. Rolling away, however, and before he could get back on his feet, and while he was still bringing his own gun to bear, he saw that Rockham was already still in place and balanced for a follow-up shot, which now could hardly be made to miss completely.

CHAPTER 14

Click.

It was odd, the way Simon Templar took a measurable fraction of time to grasp the simple reality of what had happened. The gun should have gone off with the loud bang which unsilenced examples of the species usually make. The old saw that the one which kills you is the one you never hear may be true if it kills you instantly, although there are no surviving witnesses to testify to it, but you may certainly hear the one that wounds you. Instead, this one had exploded into only this absurd, derisory little click. And there he was, alive and well, facing the man who had pulled the trigger.

And he was holding a gun of his own.

He swung it slowly up and aimed it unwaveringly at a point a few inches below Rockham's collarbone.

"That was a tough break for you," he said in his own voice. "And I've been luckier than perhaps I deserve."

Rockham smiled faintly.

"You were certainly careless. But then, so was I. I should have kept count." Rockham had paled for a moment as Simon's gun came up, but otherwise his composure was almost unruffled. "I rather think *you* did. And I think I know why you haven't shot me yet. You're out of ammunition yourself." He gestured at the revolver. "Am I right?"

"Maybe, maybe not. You've only one way to find out. And it's your kind of gamble, Rockham."

Rockham edged a step closer.

"Who are you?" He asked the question in simple curiosity, without malice.

"My name is Simon Templar. And I shall have no compunction about shooting you if you don't stay exactly where you are."

The other man stared for a moment. And then he laughed—a rich bass chuckle that was full of genuine amusement.

"The Saint! And you announced yourself literally when you arrived to—enlist. It's perfect! My congratulations. But you—you're working for these people, the authorities?"

"For the moment," Simon said, "I'm afraid I am."

"I didn't think the Saint was an organisation man."

Simon looked at him steadily and said nothing.

"If you'd come after me for yourself," Rockham said, "I might have understood."

Simon looked at him in silence for a while longer, his mind full of so many thoughts that he would not have been able to give expression to them all even if he had wanted to; and when he spoke it was to say just one thing which would have to stand for all the others which were unspoken.

"In a funny sort of way," he said slowly, "it *was* for myself that I got into this. Maybe I was wrong to take the job—I honestly don't know. But there was a man I once worked with. We went through a lot together—and when I heard that your organisation had killed him and dumped his body in the river, I had to try to do something about it. It was that simple. I don't know if you can understand that."

Rockham listened quietly, and then he said: "I believe I can. And I'd like to think I'd have done the same in your shoes."

He paused; and as before, you could almost hear the hum of dynamos in that competent brain as he searched for a fruitful line that might offer a chance of extracting some advantage from the situation.

"I'm sorry about your friend," he went on. "But nothing you can do now will bring him back." He spread his strong square hands in a gesture conveying the hopelessness of looking for resurrection. "After this, it looks as if The Squad's all washed up—thanks to your efforts. Maybe you'll think that's enough to settle the score on your friend's behalf." He pointed up the stairs. "Up there's a quarter of a million pounds' worth of human booty. All we have to do is take it. We could still get away—the jeep's outside. And we'd make a great partnership."

He looked at the Saint hopefully; but the Saint was sadly shaking his head.

"No deal, Rockham. Apart from the fact that I don't like your line of business and that partnerships don't appeal to me anyway, there are a couple of important details you've overlooked. One—about a minute ago the shooting stopped out there. Which can only mean one thing—that the cavalry, so to speak, have arrived, even if well *after* the nick of time."

He crossed carefully to the window, using a sideways crablike motion that was less elegant than functional, in that it meant he didn't take his eyes off Rockham for an instant until one brief glance out of the window was enough to confirm his inference.

"Looks like three more platoons of the Paras," he told Rockham laconically. "And your lads are herded together with their hands up. So your daring escape in the jeep would have to be—well—pretty daring."

Rockham's gaze was stony.

"And the other point I've overlooked?"

"Simply that someone's been playing come-into-my-parlour with you. This whole thing's a set-up, and has been from start to finish. You thought you'd been commissioned by the Chinese. But your Chinese—your real client—had no more to do with Peking intelligence than Christopher Robin. At least, not the way I add it up."

"Then Instrood is—"

"A fake—a plant. Like most of the rest of the cast. Instrood was bait. He was put here to tempt you—and incidentally I think there was another reason, too—one that doesn't directly concern you or The Squad."

"Then who is—was—my real client?"

The Saint saw the realisation dawning in Rockham's eyes even while he was speaking the question; and he saw how those eyes dilated and quivered like a jungle animal's when the net first falls; and he knew then beyond any kind of doubt that the man before him would never be taken alive—that he would strangle himself in the toils of the net rather than submit. And for that at least the Saint saluted Rockham, even as he went on inexorably with what he had to say.

"Your client?" he echoed lazily. "You remember I said I'd give you ten to one the girl was working for your client? I meant just that. She's an intelligence agent—British, not Chinese—and the man responsible for this whole elaborate charade is her boss. Hers, and for just a little while longer—mine. You won't know his name, but I think you should hear it at least once. It's Pelton, David Pelton."

Rockham was still standing immobile on the stairs, holding his empty revolver. The Saint, who was keeping his own gun pointed steadily at the same button of Rockham's uniform tunic and never relaxing his vigilance for an instant, knew that Rockham's efficient brain had already come to terms with his desperate situation. There was only the slightest tensing and twitching of the muscles in his jaw to betray the struggle it must have cost him to reach that hard accommodation with reality.

"I'm afraid you're done for," the Saint said, almost sympathetical. "The trap's closed. Your king's in a corner."

Rockham's pale eyes had steadied. He nodded just once, curtly, to acknowledge the facts as Simon had so starkly put them.

"Then I'm going to have to go out in a blaze of glory," he said, "and take at least one enemy piece with me if I can. I'm going to have to take that gamble on your empty gun."

He tossed his own gun on the floor with a clatter. Then, very slowly and gracefully, his lethal karate-calloused hands began to weave confusing preparations patterns in the air, as he glided a step closer to the Saint.

"Be sure of this," Rockham said. "If I hit you, I can break any of your bones like a twig." He paused, and added: "So if there's a bullet left in that gun after all—you'd better shoot to kill."

With that final statement, Rockham had come close, Simon knew, to asking for quick deliverance as a favour. And as Rockham suddenly leapt towards him, he honoured that last request, and shot him accurately through the heart.

Ruth Barnaby appeared soon after the slam of the shot had detonated into silence.

For a few moments she took in the scene impassively. Rockham was lying face down and unmoving, with the blood oozing from under him.

"It's the kind of end destiny must have marked out for him a long time ago," said the Saint quietly. "And it was self-defence for me, technically—even if he did prefer death to whatever the authorities would have done with him."

Ruth eyed him sharply.

"Don't say you're *sorry* for him?"

The Saint looked at her, and saw again that coolness in her eyes which was almost like the coldness that had stared out of Rockham's.

"No," he said. "I'm not sorry for him. He killed a lot of people —or caused a lot of people's deaths, it comes to the same thing. He deserved to die like this. But he had a kind of integrity."

"I don't understand."

"No, somehow I didn't imagine you would. Maybe it's the people you've been mixing with."

She looked puzzled for a second, and then she said: "I know you don't like Pelton's methods. But they work."

Simon assessed her dispassionately.

"Ruth," he said gently, "maybe it's not too late for you. You've been in this game long enough to see how dirty it can be, but maybe not quite long enough to accept the dirtiness as a way of life." He gripped her by the shoulders and looked searchingly into her face. "It's too late for Pelton; it's part of his existence. But not for you—I hope. Why not get out now, while you still can?"

She stared at him in amazement.

"But the service is my career. I enjoy it. And I'm ambitious. I'm still only on a low grade, but I'm going to move up."

"And all this blood-letting—the unnecessary along with the necessary—doesn't bother you?"

"Frankly, no. Not much. You can't make omelettes without breaking eggs. You may not like Pelton's methods—*our* methods— but as I've said, they work."

"Oh yes—they work, all right." The Saint's manner held no trace of his usual banter, and for once his eyes were not mocking at all but shadowed with a fury of slow-burning disgust. "A few people may incidentally get trampled on, in the course of Pelton's grand strategy, but what the hell? So two or three of Yates's men die needlessly. So what? You won't be the one to scrape their guts up off the grass or break the news to their families, and neither will Pelton!"

She shrugged.

"Whatever forces we'd had lined up, there'd probably have been a battle in which *some* men got killed or wounded."

"That may be so," Simon agreed. "But Pelton holds other people cheaper than just about anybody else I've met—and I've met some real stinkers. And I'm sorry to think of you studying under such a master."

She had never seen the Saint in such a mood of grim anger, and for a moment she seemed taken aback.

Then he asked: "What about the guards—upstairs?"

"Both unconscious," she said. "They've been clouted hard on the head. But I think they're okay, apart from the lumps."

"And Instrood?"

"I couldn't find him at all. He seems to have gone."

Simon Templar nodded slowly.

"I was afraid of that," he said. "And Nobbins, I guess, will have gone with him."

CHAPTER 15

Colonel David Pelton inspected his fingernails, made a minute and unnecessary adjustment of the alignment of a folder on his desk, and smiled with thin-lipped satisfaction.

"All in all," he said briskly to Simon Templar and Ruth Barnaby, "a highly successful operation."

"I'm glad you think so," said the Saint curtly.

"Rockham's men at Kyleham didn't put up much of a fight against the Paras we sent in there," Pelton went on. "For the time being, they've taken the place over and they're holding the Squad men there, rather than overcrowd the police cells for miles around."

The Saint eyed him coldly.

"You've no real worries then—about the whole affair?"

Pelton shook his head.

"No. It's a rough game we're in. I knew that when I started in this line. My only real concern at the moment is the expense of the whole affair. Our budgeting is—well, Civil Service. And apart from all the other costs, Rockham insisted on having a very substantial down payment for the Instrood job, and incidentally in a highly unorthodox form of currency. The Ministry treasurers weren't at all amused at having to put that sort of stake on the table. I near enough had to swear my life away to get them to play along. There'll be hell to pay if they don't get it back. That's why I shall be going down to Kyleham tomorrow with a man from Chubbs—to get into Rockham's safe."

There was no hint of a smile on the Saint's dark and now clean-shaven face, and his eyes were hard chips of blue ice.

"Never mind the funding arrangements," he said tersely. "What about Nobbins? My guess is that instead of breaking or turning Instrood, Instrood turned him."

Pelton sighed, and went through the unnecessary straightening motions with the folder again.

"Poor old Nobbins. I'm afraid he rather went to pieces when he discovered the truth about Instrood. We picked the pair of them up near Hounslow. Nobbins thought he was on his way to the Chinese Embassy. There's no doubt Instrood did a good job."

"That's what you call it?"

Pelton spread his well-manicured hands half-apologetically.

"Simon—it had to be done." He glanced at Ruth for support, and she nodded vigorously. "We can't afford sentimentality in the service. The fact is, Nobbins had been showing certain signs of instability for some months. The weakness, if it was there, had to be brought out in the open."

Simon laughed ironically.

"And if it wasn't there—it had to be created."

"Not exactly. But I agree that the technique used with him was calculated to expose—to precipitate, even—a lack of dedication that may have been only latent."

"So you started by softening him up, putting him under maximum stress. You packed him off to The Squad, and with a cover so ramshackle it was pretty well bound to have holes blown through it within weeks if not days of his arrival there."

Pelton canted his head over at that birdlike angle, and his small dark eyes glittered.

"Nobbins was useful in the role. And it was—shall we say not inconvenient that the job put him under a certain amount of pressure."

"You used him as a pawn in your game with Rockham—callously and with infinite calculation," said the Saint. He stabbed the air with an accusing forefinger. "You used him in a cold-blooded gambit. And it didn't matter to you whether your opponent accepted it or not, because you were into a winning line of play either way. Whether he shaped up or not—you'd come out with something to the good. Rockham and his Squad were your main objective, but you could combine settling your doubts about Nobbins in the same operation."

The Saint was warming to his subject, in so far as it was the sort of subject he could think about in terms of warming to.

"If they tumbled to Nobbins—well, in that case you were rid of a job, and the sacrifice would probably strengthen your hand, like all the best gambits, in the rest of the game. For instance, another of your pieces might well be able to operate more freely. This one." Simon pointed to himself. "Having rooted out one infiltrator, Rockham wouldn't be expecting a second one to be already installed. But if on the other hand they didn't tumble to him—then he'd be collecting some mildly useful information while he was there. And all the time he was obligingly reducing himself to a jelly, to a state of full susceptibility to the next trial he had to go through—the next phase of your plan."

"As I've said, he had to be tested." Pelton shrugged.

"Or was it tempted? You know as well as I do that there's a sensible ordinance in this country that prohibits the police from inciting a man to commit a crime in order to charge him with it. I've no doubt there are a hundred and one more or less subtle ways of acting the *agent provocateur* in that sense without technically breaking that law, but at least it helps prevent official incitement of the more blatant kinds. I'm only sorry—for Nobbins's sake —that a similar bridle doesn't apply here."

Again the Saint's forefinger stabbed out in Pelton's direction.

"But it doesn't," he went on. "So you baited your double hook —Instrood, or whatever his real name is—for Rockham and for Nobbins. You assigned Nobbins to the interrogation, and you briefed Instrood to go to work on him—to play on his weaknesses in any way possible. I suppose Nobbins was made to feel he'd be more highly valued in Peking than here—especially if he'd helped their precious Instrood to get back to them."

Pelton nodded. He gazed at Simon with quiet perceptiveness.

"Something of the sort," he agreed. "I rather gathered from Ruth here that you'd managed to work it out for yourself. I'm most impressed, Simon, most impressed. Mind you, she herself had guessed most of it by this evening."

"It wasn't too difficult," she said modestly. "When you sent Bert Nobbins into The Squad, at first I thought just what he was meant to think. I knew he'd asked for something different a few times—a more active assignment. And now something had come up, and you were giving him the chance he'd been asking for. He wanted to do it, even if he *was* petrified from start to finish. But then, when you gave him the job of interrogating Instrood, I began to wonder what you were up to. I knew you couldn't really leave a genuinely important interrogation to him. But after I'd worked it out, I must say I thought you'd been extremely clever."

Pelton favoured her with one of his thin smiles; but the Saint's expression was stony.

"I thought it was clever, too," he said evenly. "But the reaction it produces in me, as you've gathered, isn't one of admiration. Nor do I propose to bore you with a detailed recital of the thought processes I followed in tuning myself in to your unsavoury machinations. My reasoning was probably much the same as Ruth's, anyhow, and she presents it with so much more flattery than I ever could."

The Saint stood up, and looked hard at the two of them for what he earnestly hoped would be the last time.

"You already know," he said, "that I'd never have agreed to get mixed up in any of this if I'd known then what I know now. But I did get myself into it, and I've done what you asked. And now I'm going away to wash the nasty taste out of my mouth. As you said—it's a rough game, Pelton. And I'm used to rough games. But your kind of rough game isn't mine. I'm too sorry for the losers, the exploited—the little men, the cheated and chiselled of the world. Men like Nobbins."

He paused, with his hand on the doorknob; and because he had reached the end of that episode in his life, and was about to return thankfully to being wholly his own man again, something of the old light had already begun to come back into his dark buccaneering face. There was a parting shot he couldn't resist.

"There are many words, Pelton," he said quietly, "for what you are. But let me put it this way. You and your job may have been made for each other, but there's another vocation which I'm afraid you've missed. You would have been very good on the land . . . if only they'd thought up a way of *spreading* you!"

And the Saint shut the door and went out into the cool London night.

For a time, which may have been ten minutes or twenty or
thirty, he wandered by the Thames, along the embankment near
Westminster Bridge, gazing at the sluggish current of the dark
waters which symbolised for him bitter adventure that would soon
be only a memory like all the others. That was a consolation.
There were few of those adventures that he regretted, but this was
one; and the sooner it became a distant recollection, the better.

But there were other consolations, too; and a little more of that
light came back into his face and into his mind, pushing aside the
dark clouds that had formed there, when he thought of the return
trip he would make to Kyleham that night. There was a girl there,
he remembered, with summer in her hair and autumn in her eyes,
and who drove a tractor with a zest that spoke volumes about her
in itself, who had probably never even dreamt that such a dirty
tricks department as Pelton's even existed.

But before looking her up, as he had promised, he still had his
way over the wall of Rockham's former camp; and he felt reasonably confident that he could get into Kyleham House, and open
Rockham's safe, and close it again, and get back out of the
grounds, leaving no evidence of his return, long before Pelton got
there with his man from Chubbs.